All of a sudden she was fighting to keep her distance from him, and it was getting harder and harder. She wasn't sure when it had happened. Just little moments from after the crash, when he'd given her that extra bit of support. An embrace.

But she thought the big moment had been when he'd suggested she walk behind him, to shade herself from the sun, and that he carry her bag. The idea was sweet and thoughtful—useless, because the sun had been overhead, but still there had been the constant view of sinewy ripples of muscle in his shoulders through his shirt, and of strong, determined thighs in his jeans as he'd walked ahead of her.

And just now, when he'd reached down with those big, capable hands. He was supposed to be city-soft and reliant on her, but she knew if she let him he'd lift her to the top of the rock with no effort. That was when she'd got scared. When she'd started to realise he was occupying too much of her mind space.

A mother to five sons, **Fiona McArthur** is an Australian midwife who loves to write. Mills & Boon® Medical™ Romance gives Fiona the scope to write about all the wonderful aspects of adventure, romance, medicine and midwifery that she feels so passionate about—as well as an excuse to travel! So now that the boys are older, her husband Ian and youngest son Rory are off with Fiona to meet new people, see new places, and have wonderful adventures. Fiona's website is at www.fionamcarthur.com

Recent titles by the same author:

MIDWIFE IN A MILLION
PREGNANT MIDWIFE: FATHER NEEDED
  Lyrebird Lake Maternity
THE MIDWIFE'S LITTLE MIRACLE
  Lyrebird Lake Maternity
THE MIDWIFE'S NEW-FOUND FAMILY
  Lyrebird Lake Maternity
THEIR SPECIAL-CARE BABY

THE MIDWIFE AND THE MILLIONAIRE

BY
FIONA McARTHUR

First published in Great Britain 2010
Harlequin Mills & Boon Limited,
Eton House, 18-24 Paradise Road, Richmond, Surrey TW9 1SR

© Fiona McArthur 2010

ISBN: 978 0 263 21369 0

THE MIDWIFE
AND THE
MILLIONAIRE

WITH THANKS TO:

Glenn at Heliworks, for his help with helicopters
and moments of unusual interest.

To Fiona, the guide at the Bungle Bungles, who shared
her knowledge and enthusiasm for an amazing place.

And Annie, for being a natural-born teacher
and one of my wonderful Maytone friends.

CHAPTER ONE

ANOTHER squat boab tree dropped its leaves as Sophie Sullivan drove past, a sure sign the wet season was nearly over. She sounded her car horn at the frilled-neck lizard basking in the middle of the dirt track and he reared on hind legs, spread his neck frill and hissed until he seemed much more than he really was.

Typical male.

At least the craggy red mountains that embraced her were true, she thought, as she drove towards the boulder-strewn river—that range was a dear part of home.

Home: far north Western Australia, the Kimberleys and a place blissfully away from the city and men who shed lies like the boab shed leaves.

Even the dusty Gibb River Road looked attractive until she saw the vehicle parked by the Pentecost and the motionless man beside the sluggish water.

More crocodile fodder. She sighed—travellers caused her no end of concern, especially ones who hovered for long periods at the edge of the crocodile-inhabited rivers.

The tourists parked by the river because of the view to the Cockburn Range across the ochre plains. Locals used the designated parking area at the top of the hill, well away from the water.

She pulled up next to the expensive all-terrain vehicle and wound down her window. 'You OK, there?'

The man didn't answer. He must've heard her truck. She was ten feet away from him. Careless *and* rude, she thought and narrowed her eyes. Finally he turned his head and glanced at her dismissively. 'Fine, thanks.'

He was big—Sophie couldn't help but notice—bigger than her brother, Smiley, who topped six-two, and this guy was very nicely muscled so he'd be a mouthful for any croc, but he was too close and too stationary in a dangerous spot. It would be a shame to waste the body, she thought dispassionately, and with the new knowledge from Brand-name Brad she could have done without, it would be a waste of the designer jeans and Rolex watch.

Congratulations were in order for her immunity from the male species. A hard-won but valuable lesson.

Sophie bit back another sigh. How did you tell someone to get back in their vehicle when they blatantly ignored you?

'You've seen the warnings?' She looked at the sign herself, read it under her breath even. 'Crocodiles Inhabit This Area. Keep Away from the Edge. Do Not Enter the Water.' But her reading it didn't make him face her. In fact, no further response to her at all.

Grrr. Spare me from arrogant males. Despite the flags that waved from the man to say go away, she tried one more time. 'About the crocodiles here?'

'Yes, thanks.' Far less cordial and this time he shifted his feet so he faced her. 'I'm just passing through.'

'You'll pass right through a croc,' she said drily. 'I lost my darling dog in a spot like this once.' And still had nightmares about the tragedy her lack of concentration had caused.

Then he looked directly at her. He wasn't to-die-for handsome, really, but he had those dark, dark lashes and an intense gaze that held her, effortlessly, until he dropped the connection as easily as he'd reeled her in. The trumpet call. *Danger*, and not from crocodiles. Her skin prickled.

'I'm sorry to hear about your pet.' He glanced back at the river before he looked again at her, to assess if she'd be a nuisance by the look of it, and Sophie could feel the warmth of the sun beat in the window, or she hoped that explained the heat.

Best not to become entangled in another look so she concentrated on a small scar on his chin that made him less imposing—more vulnerable, which was a funny thing to think about a stranger, but his mouth… She had a sudden ridiculous urge to see those lips smile.

Sophie searched for the question she'd asked.

He coughed and she looked up in time to see him roll his eyes, obviously used to stunned mullet expressions on passing females, and he didn't bother to hide the sigh. 'If I get attacked by a croc because I had to talk to you I'm going to be extremely unhappy.'

Sophie blinked. What the heck was she doing? So much for immunity! She obviously needed a booster shot against this guy, so leaving was a great idea. 'Right, then. Your funeral.' For the first time in ten years Sophie crunched the gears as she slipped her vehicle into reverse.

Levi Pearson turned back to contemplate the spot where his father had been taken five months ago. Or had he been pushed and the crocodile only secondary to his demise? He'd find out.

That tiny whiff of suspicion, something only he seemed to have sniffed, was the reason he'd flown up here after the wet season and why he'd asked his stubbornly determined sister not to mention their proper connection to Xanadu. That and the fact the other consultant he worked with had recommended a holiday for the tenth time in the past two years.

As soon as he'd confirmed or dismissed the concept of foul play he'd get her the hell out of downtown nowheresville and back to Sydney. The manager here was more than capable of running Xanadu, and Levi didn't need another burden, but he'd discovered a motive he couldn't dismiss.

Lord knew the original owners of the station had enough reason to hate his family if the stories of his father were true.

He took his eye off the bank and risked a glance at the blonde woman's four-wheel-drive vehicle as it ploughed through the river away from him. Nothing else mattered. Hadn't for a long while. Definitely not a pair of concerned blue eyes under two stern eyebrows. Above a lush little mouth. He frowned. She'd been an officious little thing but strangely intriguing.

Still, he'd read the population of the Kimberley region was about thirty thousand people in an area slightly bigger than Germany and it was the last place he'd ever settle. So, he should be safe from bumping into her again. He didn't need the complication of fleeting sexual attraction to a cowgirl.

A stealthy splash to the left of where he stood had his attention firmly back on the water and Levi took a few steps towards the vehicle he'd borrowed from the resort. Probably better not to get eaten and give her the chance to say *I told you so*.

He could feel the twitch of his lips at the thought, along with surprise at the idea of smiling, something he hadn't done much of in the past year or two, and climbed back into his vehicle.

Nearly two hours later Sophie swerved around another pothole and the old four-wheel drive bounced off the thousandth corrugation on her way to Jabiru Station Township. They'd grade the road soon now the rain had stopped. She gritted her teeth to stop the jarring. Almost home.

Funnily enough, she wasn't tired. Hadn't been since the Pentecost. She didn't want to think about the man at the river any more. It had been one of those moments in time when you catch another person's eye and, for a second or two, glances tangle and reverberate, and then you both look away and the moment passes.

Except the moment seemed to last an eternity and she was still waiting for it to pass.

It had been one of those moments. Just a stranger. With great eyes. And a great body. And a great mouth. Even in the firm line, she remembered, his mouth had hinted at a fullness and dangerous curve that made her wonder how he'd got the scar. She hoped some hot-blooded woman had thrown a plate at him. Her lips twitched but she pulled them back into line. He'd looked like everything she didn't want in a man.

Rude, definitely.

Stupid, obviously. She frowned. He didn't look stupid; actually, he'd looked fearsomely intelligent. So not stupid, maybe reckless. She didn't want that either, did she? No way.

Worst of all, he'd had the trappings of her ex. Stinking, selfishly, blatantly wealthy. Like Dr Brad Gale. The liar. She was finished with doctors and liars and people who thought they could buy you. And serve you a prenuptial at the same time.

She was glad to be home, in a place where people said what they meant and didn't string you along. Where she could be useful to those who needed her, and not as some decorative arm hanging, and definitely not confined to answering only when spoken to.

Sophie did wonder if her poor brother had become used to his bachelor ways while she'd been away. He'd looked surprised when she'd arrived to move back into her own room, even if 'Shortest engagement in history,' was all he'd said.

She drove through the tiny Jabiru Station Township—mostly pubs and boarded buildings—to their house, a modest timber residence with bull-nosed verandas on all sides and a tiny dry garden. Neat and comfortable, in the same state of disrepair as they'd inherited it from their parents, who'd inherited it from her father's parents after Granddad did that bad thing.

A place where Smiley could save every cent for his dream station, like the one his grandfather had been tricked out of in a card game all those years ago. Against a man who'd lied.

Not that Smiley lusted after Xanadu. He'd his own plans for a different station that accounted for his cattle having to be lodged all over the Kimberley while he saved for the land, but it irked Sophie that her own father and now Smiley had to scrimp so hard to make their way in the place they were born.

'You must've loaded the cattle early, because I didn't see the road train on the way in,' she said as she rounded the veranda, then stopped. He had someone with him.

Her brother's drawl seemed more noticeable, which was saying something, as his normal speech defined the word *leisurely*. 'Sophie.' He looked at her, and then indicated the petite dark-haired woman beside him. 'This is Odette. From Sydney. She's having a baby, and in the area for a week or so, and wanted to meet a midwife in case she had any problems.'

Sophie held out her hand and shook the young woman's perfectly manicured fingers. Nice expensive watch. Brad had bought her one just like it. She'd left it in Perth.

Sophie bit back the thought. He'd made her judgemental and that wasn't like her—or hadn't been before she'd tripped off to Perth for her midwifery. She needed to get her new prejudice under control. Wealthy tourists kept a lot of people in jobs around here.

'Nice to meet you, Odette. Welcome to Jabiru Station Township. You been waiting long?'

'I flew in an hour ago.' Her coral-coloured lips tilted as she smiled. She had a sweet face, Sophie thought, and well made up, which was interesting as the heat usually melted foundation around here. 'Guess I should have rung first but I thought the clinic was open.'

Sophie looked across the street to the old homestead that'd been turned into the clinic. 'I've been visiting an Aboriginal community. It's "women's health" day. Just takes a few hours to cover the distance around here.'

'So Smiley was explaining.' She looked shyly up at Sophie's brother. Goofily, Smiley actually smiled back, an occurrence that was so rare it had derived his nickname. Sophie felt herself frown. She'd never seen him look like that. Or be much into explaining anything. She'd be lucky to get a dozen words out of him on a normal morning.

'Odette flew herself in a chopper,' he said.

Impressive. 'You're a pilot? Wow.' And very pregnant, but she didn't say it.

Odette shrugged with a smile. 'I do it for fun. You're a midwife. Wow.'

Sophie had to laugh. 'I do that for fun too. My friend, Kate, the other midwife, flies her own plane from Jabiru Homestead.'

Odette exuded good nature and Sophie couldn't help liking her. 'So you're having a baby? And want a check-up? Come across to the clinic. Was there something you were worried about?'

Odette turned and smiled at Sophie's brother. 'Thanks, Smiley. I hope I get to see you again.'

He nodded and tipped his hat. The two women crossed the road and Odette looked back. 'Your brother's a handsome man.'

Sophie blinked. She'd never thought about it. He was just...Smiley. 'If he's not in the house he's got an Akubra on so I don't often see his face. I guess I still see skinned knees and freckles.'

'I didn't see any of those.' Odette sounded almost dreamy and Sophie grimaced. City-rich women and Smiley did not mix.

'Is it your husband's helicopter?' Not very subtle.

'I don't have a husband.' Odette was no fool and she

met Sophie's eyes without a flicker. 'The father of my baby is dead.'

Bummer, for more reasons than one, Sophie thought. Was she being judgemental again? 'Sorry for being nosy.'

'That's OK. Better to get it out in the open anyway. He wasn't a nice man,' Odette went on. 'And the chopper belongs to the resort where I'm staying.'

'That would be Xanadu, then.' It wasn't a question. Xanadu. Now an ultra-high-end resort a hundred kilometres away, as the chopper flew, that catered for a Kimberley adventure in five-star luxury. Private suites, fine wine and cuisine, and escorted tours with private sittings in the hot springs and gorges. They'd turned it into a wilderness park with a few token cattle. Not like in Grandfather's day. 'I've never known them to lend the chopper before.'

Odette shrugged. 'I just asked the manager.' She looked across at Sophie. 'I could take you and Smiley up for a fly if you want.'

'Thanks, but maybe another time. Should you be flying when you're pregnant?'

'You sound like my brother.'

Now why did she suddenly think of the man at the river? 'Don't suppose he's a big bloke, scar on his chin, not into smiling.' The one who was 'just passing through.'

'You've met Levi?'

'Levi?' It seemed he was another person who was happy to bend the truth. As opposed to the straightforward people from around here who didn't lie. 'Yep. Guess I have. He was at the Pentecost River crossing.' Sophie didn't say *a little too close to the water* because she didn't want to worry Odette. She shrugged. 'I warned him about the crocodiles.'

Odette pursed her lips for a moment, then visibly pushed away whatever had caused the look. 'He knows about the crocodiles. But thank you. Levi is a good guy, just forgotten how to have fun.'

And too attractive, and Sophie needed to talk about something new because she had the feeling anything else she learnt about him wouldn't help her forget.

'So when's your baby due, Odette?'

'A month.'

Sophie fought to keep her jaw from dropping but she had another look. Surely too small. Maybe Odette had it all tucked away. 'I'd say your brother was right and you shouldn't be flying. Where's your mother?'

'She died when I was a kid.' Oops, Sophie thought. Another foot-in-mouth question.

Luckily Odette didn't seem worried. 'Levi brought me up. Our father ran off with another woman when I was young. That's why Levi's serious. He's been the man of the house for a lot of years.'

Too much information. Not hearing this. 'OK.' Sophie pushed open the door and they went into the small exam room. 'How about I check your blood pressure, feel your tummy and have a listen to your baby's heart rate? If it's OK with you I'll photocopy your antenatal card. Then if you have any worries I can talk you through most of it on the phone.'

Odette grinned. 'This is like booking into a spare hospital.'

Sophie smiled back. 'Except we don't deliver babies here, only the unexpected ones.' She gestured to the chair beside her desk. 'Have a seat.'

Odette settled herself and held out her arm. 'That's OK. We'll probably be back in Sydney in a few days anyway.'

Maybe that justifies as passing through and he didn't technically lie. Though what the heck was he doing bringing someone this pregnant away from home?

Sophie wrapped the cuff around Odette's arm and pumped it up, then let it down. She unhooked the stethoscope from her ears and smiled. 'Blood pressure's perfect. One ten on sixty.' She indicated the footstool beside the examination table. 'If you can climb up there we'll see where this baby of yours is hiding.'

Odette chuckled. 'Everyone says I'm small but I was only five pounds when I was born. The ultrasound said it's a boy.'

Sophie draped a thin sheet over the lower half of Odette's body and Odette lifted her shirt. 'A boy. Wow. Nice tummy.' Sophie was serious. Odette's abdomen curved up in a perfect small hill, brown and smooth, and the baby shifted a body part into a small point as Sophie laughed. 'He's waving.'

Odette slid her hand over the point and the baby

subsided as if trained. 'My baby's no sloth. Moves heaps, especially at night.'

'Women tend to feel their babies at night because they're not busy like they are in the daytime. They say the baby already has a rhythm so if he's awake a lot at night you might be in for some sleep deprivation.'

'I don't mind.' Odette smiled dreamily. 'I can't wait.'

I hope you do, Sophie thought, as she measured the mound of Odette's belly and, taking into account the petite mother, the measurements confirmed Odette's estimated due date.

She slid the hand-held Doppler over the area she'd palpated as the baby's shoulder and the sound of the baby's heart rate filled the room. They both listened and their eyes met in mutual acknowledgement of the wonder of childbearing. 'There you go,' Sophie said, as she turned off the Doppler. 'One hundred and forty beats a minute and just as perfect as his mother.'

She helped Odette sit up. 'Everything looks great.'

'Thanks, Sophie. I feel better just talking to you.' Odette climbed down and smoothed her clothes. 'How much do I owe you?'

Sophie shook her head. 'I didn't do anything. Free service. Anyone can walk in and get the same.'

'You and Smiley should come over to Xanadu on the weekend and have dinner with my brother and me. Our treat. As a thank-you for this.' She gestured to the examination couch. 'I could come and get you in the chopper. Or Levi could.'

Lord, no. And she thought they were going in a day or two? It was only Monday. She walked her to the door. 'Thanks, Odette, but the weather's still too unsettled for me to fly—I'm a chicken in the air—and I don't know what Smiley's planned. I've only just moved back from Perth.'

'Sure. I'll ring later in the week.' Odette stopped and turned back with a new idea. 'If you're not keen on flying, you could stay overnight and drive back the next day. In fact, that sounds more fun anyway.'

Sophie felt she was being directed by a small determined whirly wind, like the one that was lifting leaves outside her window and the one inside her chest when she thought of staying anywhere near Odette's brother. 'I'll mention it to Smiley.' Not.

Odette pulled a gold compact from her bag, flicked open the mirror and touched up her lipstick. Not something Sophie did regularly out here in the bush and the thought made her smile to herself.

Odette snapped shut the compact. 'What's your brother's real name?'

Sophie had to think for a moment. 'William.'

Odette nodded as if she liked it. 'I think I'll call him William.'

'It's been a while since anybody has.' Now where was this going? Nowhere, she hoped. 'He may not even remember it.'

'Even more reason to,' Odette said cryptically.

* * *

That afternoon, Levi poured his sister a chilled juice and himself a cold beer before he moved to look over the veranda at the gorge below. Then her words sank in. He turned back to her. 'You what?'

'I invited William and Sophie to stay over for a night on the weekend. The midwife and her brother. To have dinner and drive home the next day.'

He'd strangle her. 'Did I mention we didn't want to draw attention until I find out if anyone around here hated our father enough to push him into that river?'

Odette crossed her arms and lent them over her large tummy. 'Hated him more than you?'

Levi shook his head. 'I didn't hate him. I didn't respect him. That's all.'

He fully intended to sign the ownership he'd unexpectedly inherited back over to his sister, another baffling development his estranged father had left for him, when they'd all expected Odette to benefit by the resort automatically.

Odette rolled her eyes. 'Because you've just found out he's had another son to another woman. Humph.' She returned to topic. 'Besides, they wouldn't know anything about Father's accident. Sophie's only just moved back from Perth and William is—' she paused and her mouth curved '—just William. He hasn't a mean bone in his body.'

He flung his hand out towards the view. 'We don't know that. Your new best friends. You've met them, what, once?'

'You've met her too.' Odette sat forward as he frowned.

He'd done his part. He'd avoided meeting anyone. Not likely. 'When?'

'She said she'd met you by the river—' Odette didn't quite poke out her tongue but he knew that look '—this afternoon.' A winning point.

The little honey in the car? The last person he needed to be exposed to, as she seemed lodged like an annoying bindii from the grass in his memory bank. 'Blonde ponytail? Nice, um, features?'

Odette coughed and he couldn't help the curve of his own lips. He really didn't have socialising on his agenda on this trip. He needed to go home; he'd already been away past his expectations, and his theatre list would be a mile long.

His sister would be the death of him. He sighed. Too late now. 'So why can't we fly them in and out? That way they don't have to stay.'

Odette shrugged. 'Sophie doesn't fancy the chopper.'

Chicken, eh? Good. Though she hadn't seemed a shrinking violet. 'Maybe she wouldn't mind so much if the pilot didn't look like she was going to break her waters any moment?'

Odette flapped her hand at him. 'You're too used to your own way. Let me worry about me.'

CHAPTER TWO

Five days later

'I DON'T know how you talked me into this.' Sophie glared at her brother.

Smiley kept his eyes on the road. 'You've been twitchy all week.'

'And you've been moonstruck like a big old cow.'

Smiley turned to look at her briefly but didn't say anything.

It was disappointing. A bit of a spat might have taken her mind off the nerves that were building ridiculously at the thought of meeting the brooding rich man again. She was even avoiding his name in her thoughts. How ridiculous.

Unable to get a rise out of Smiley she turned to watch the scenery flash by. The overhanging escarpment of the Cockburn ranges in the distance ran along the right side of the vehicle and the stumpy gums and dry grass covered the plains to the left before they soared into more ochre-red cliffs that tinged purple as the sun set.

Sophie knew the darkening gorges hid pockets of tangled rainforest and deep cold pools like the dread she could feel at meeting him again.

But the stands of thick and thin trees made her smile. She'd missed the pot bellies of the grey-trunked boabs the most while she'd been in Perth.

'Why don't you like Odette?' Smiley was stewing. Something in his voice warned her not to be flippant.

'Who wouldn't like Odette?' she said carefully. 'She seems lovely. I just don't want you hurt when she flies back to Sydney.'

Smiley frowned at the road ahead and Sophie winced at his displeasure. Now that was something she'd very rarely encountered and she didn't like it. 'I'm sorry, Smiley. I have no right to judge your friends. I think Odette's great. I just can't see her as an outback girl and I can't see you in the city. But it's none of my business.'

'Thank you.' His voice was dry and the two words were a statement. Thanking her for agreeing it was none of her business.

Oops. She really had upset her brother and that was something she'd never consciously do. Since her parents had died she'd become used to bossing Smiley around, giving her opinion, and he'd never seemed to mind.

Obviously she'd crossed the line with Odette. She'd just have to button her lip and trust Smiley's instincts.

It would've been easier if she'd sent him to Xanadu

on his own though. She had the feeling her trepidation for Smiley was tied up in the trepidation she held for herself with Odette's mysterious brother.

Smiley turned off the main dirt road onto the red dust of the track through the scrub. They splashed through several watercourses and wound through the ochre-coloured hills until they turned into the Private Property, No Entry sign that hid the homestead.

'Welcoming,' she mumbled, and Smiley glanced at her.

'You've met the brother?'

'Briefly.' She could be just as taciturn. She didn't expand her explanation and Smiley didn't ask again. Then the homestead came into view.

Xanadu Homestead was a long low building, and she'd been too young to remember visiting in her grandparents' day. Apparently now it had been divided up into luxury suites, if what Sophie had heard was right, perched on the edge of the escarpment above the river that flowed beneath it.

The main building faced into the sunset which glowed deep red as it faded. Nice place to holiday if you had the platinum or even a black credit card, but not when you were eight months pregnant. Why would Odette and her brother come here now?

At least the thought gave her something else to concentrate on as they drew up at the house. She wondered what the other guests would think of outsiders being invited to invade their sanctuary. What month was this?

April. The resort would only just have opened for the season anyway.

Odette swayed onto the main entrance portico in a muslin caftan that must have cost a bomb, and Sophie wondered how she could still be graceful when she was supposed to be awkward in the last month of pregnancy. Sophie glanced at Smiley and judging by his face he'd just seen the Holy Grail.

Sophie sighed and felt for the handle to climb out of the truck when her door moved away from her grasp.

'Welcome to Xanadu.' Levi held out his hand and Sophie wasn't sure if he wanted to shake hers or help her from the vehicle. Where'd he come from? She'd been hoping to see him from a distance and get her face straight.

She resisted the urge to snap her hand back to her side and forced herself to let him take her fingers. Initially cool, the strength in his fingers surprised her, but not as much as the feeling of insidious connection, a frisson of ridiculous warmth that passed between them and echoed the impact of his eyes. There was something she'd deny with her last breath.

No. She hadn't felt a thing. So why rub her hand surreptitiously behind her back? And why did he look down at her with one enigmatic eyebrow raised as if he'd been surprised as well?

Then Odette was dancing around the car like an elegant puppy as she looked adoringly up at Smiley, and Levi left her to shake Smiley's hand.

'It's so good to see you, William.' Odette flashed a smile at Sophie before she looked back at Smiley and captured his hand. Odette tugged his fingers to make him follow her. 'This is my brother, Levi,' she said dismissively. 'Now, come and see the place.'

'William' looked back at Sophie, who managed a tiny smiling shrug that said she'd be fine.

'My sister can be impetuous,' Levi said grimly.

'My brother can't.' She watched Smiley leap up the stairs after Odette. 'Or I didn't think he could.'

Levi lifted one eyebrow sardonically. 'Welcome to Xanadu. I'll send someone for the bags when we get inside.'

Sophie glanced in the back of the truck. 'Actually, we're used to carrying our own.'

He inclined his head. 'But I'd be offended. Please come in.'

The bags weren't worth standing out here with him so she turned resolutely towards the entrance. He went on. 'The resort's not technically opened for the season and we have the run of the place.'

'Well, that's very nice.' But she couldn't help thinking, How the heck did you do that? They must know the owners extremely well or have unlimited funds. Best not go there. 'When does it open?'

He glanced at the sky. 'Depends on the weather and the state of the roads, though apparently next week, if all continues well.'

She slanted a look across at him. 'I guess you and Odette will be gone by then.'

Another enigmatic brow rose. 'Trying to get rid of us?'

They crossed the gravel drive to the stairs and she paused. 'You did say you were passing through. A week ago,' she said calmly.

'I lied.' Straightfaced, no remorse.

Sophie blinked. She'd known he was dangerous. Like sniffing the briny scent before a storm. Her instincts had been right. He was trouble. She started walking again, faster now, but he kept pace. 'People don't tend to do that up here.' Liar like Brad.

His eyes narrowed as if he sensed some history there. 'Necessity can make liars out of us all.'

She could feel her lip curl. 'So some people say.'

He looked across at her and no doubt he could see her distaste. She hoped so. 'Had a bad experience with a man, have you?'

'I think I'll look for my brother.' She turned away but before she could take a step he caught her hand again and she pulled up short to look back at him with raised eyebrows, actually astounded that he would invade her intimate space.

Maybe he didn't know that people from the bush— used to wide-open spaces and few people—didn't do space invasion well. Smiley tended to wave at people rather than shake their hands. Not like those from the city, who were used to people brushing up against them in elevators and on city streets.

He let go. This time she didn't hide that she rubbed her hand.

'I apologise, Sophie.' To give him his due he looked as confused as she felt. 'We seem to have got off on the wrong foot. Twice.' Those deadly lips of his were as devastating in an almost smile as she'd imagined. Damn him.

'Now why do we rub each other the wrong way, do you think?'

No way was Sophie going there. She looked him up and down. Coolly, she hoped. 'I'm not interested in rubbing anyone at all.'

His almost smile, which she decided was forced anyway, departed and he nodded. 'Let's go in, then.' He gestured with his hand for her to precede him, but he didn't touch her. And she didn't thank him for the courtesy because she could feel his eyes on her back uncomfortably the whole way up the steps. And he was still in her space.

Levi watched her attempt to walk sedately ahead of him; they both knew something had happened. He wanted to come up beside her and put his hand on the small of her back—lay claim, in fact—and he crunched his fingers into his palm to stop from reaching out. She'd invaded his head with the tiny bit he'd seen the other day but in full-blown glory she took his breath away.

Her dress was simple and blue but smoothed the slender line of her back and hips as she swayed in front of him and her legs were bare and brown and long enough to dream about. This was crazy. She smoked, just by walking in front of him.

It felt as if a wire from one of the fences dragged him along in her wake, and there was a tautness he could see in her shoulders that said she wasn't comfortable either.

He didn't know what it was. Apart from totally impractical and heinously inconvenient…but then again the travel agent had quoted the Kimberleys as a destination of adventure. Suddenly he was thinking of a side tour of a different sort.

He ushered her, with great restraint and no contact, through to the veranda where they all shared the sunset, or at least her brother and his sister shared it; he and Sophie separately observed. Maybe not even that because he wasn't looking at hills bathed in purple.

He'd always had a thing about women with long necks and hers flowed like an orchid to her throat. He'd bet her skin felt as soft as a petal. He shifted his scrutiny away from temptation and looked higher. He couldn't see her eyes from where he stood but he knew they were blue. Like her dress. High cheekbones, snubby nose that should have just been snubby but turned out deliciously cute, and those lips. He reefed his eyes away and took a long swallow of his beer. Who was he and what had happened to the normal, sane, over-worked man who'd arrived last week?

Shame it wasn't prehistoric times because dragging her off to his cave looked mighty appealing to him at this moment. And no one had appealed for a while. He'd better find something to stay focused on, something apart from how to get her into bed.

'Odette tells me you're a midwife,' he said, and now he could see her eyes. Her pupils were big and dark and he'd read somewhere that was a sign of arousal. He hoped so 'cause he was sure his eyes would be all pupil to his lashes.

She ran her finger around the rim of her glass and even that tiny movement made him swallow. 'And community nurse, and anything else that needs medical attention,' she said.

He almost wished he was sick. 'Sounds diverse. It must be a heavy workload.' He watched her face light up.

'I enjoy it,' she said. 'Love it, in fact. Now it has the added dimension of meeting people like Odette who'd benefit from access to a midwife.'

Passion for her job. Bless her. He used to have that. Now he didn't even want to talk about work. 'Odette said you've just returned from Perth.'

He felt the cold breeze and even her pupils constricted until her eyes were light blue again. She jutted her chin and he regretted the question. Obviously bad choice of conversation and a major setback. Probably a good thing.

'Yes. It's great to be home.' Such a cold voice, so different than when she'd spoken of work.

She put her glass down and turned to his sister. 'The view is wonderful, Odette.' Sophie pretended to be absorbed and tried to fade Levi into the background. She didn't want to think about Perth and the fool she'd made of herself there. Though it served as a reminder not to be foolish here. Just because externally Odette's brother was hard to ignore, internally he'd be the same as Brad. He'd already shown his arrogant, untruthful side. Rich, callous, oblivious to hurting others. And she'd promised she'd never become that vulnerable again.

She just wished he'd stop studying her. She could feel him watching. Could feel the brush of his analytical study as if she were some strange species he hadn't figured out yet and it made her want to think of some witty, slash-cutting thing to make him back off. But of course she couldn't think of something. No doubt tonight in bed it would be there on her tongue.

Well, he could look, but she refused to squirm. He'd be used to city women falling all over him but he'd come to the wrong place for that. Here a woman wanted a man with more to his repertoire than looking good.

'So what do you do, Levi?' Apart from watching me. Not that she was interested.

'I have a business in Sydney.'

City slicker. She'd bet it wasn't a physical job because his hands looked too clean. She wasn't going to comment, even mentally, on his obvious fitness.

He raised his eyebrows. 'You have a very expressive face. By the curl of your lip I'm surprised you think I do anything?'

'Perhaps.' She abandoned the subject. If he didn't want to tell her, then that was fine. The less she knew about him, the better. She turned her shoulder further away from him.

'My sister tells me you don't like helicopters much.'

Politeness meant she had to turn back. No doubt he would see her reluctance and maybe then he'd leave her alone. 'Nothing personal to helicopters, I don't like to fly.'

He shifted his body so she was lined up with him again. 'Shame, then. A pilot's licence would be useful with the distances they have out here.'

Like Kate and her plane. She'd never feel comfortable enough to do that. 'My friend flies. I'll do without.'

He acknowledged her aversion with a flick of his hand. 'It's a different world, immediate, stunning, and even I admit this country is spectacular from the air.'

She felt her hackles rise and she sipped her drink before she answered to damp down her desire to demand he appreciate her home. 'The Kimberleys are spectacular from the ground as well.'

He put his glass down. 'I've offended you again.'

'The bush is not for everyone.' She shrugged, thankfully.

'And you're happy about that?'

It seemed she couldn't cause him offence. 'There are advantages.' Well, at least they were conversing in a fairly normal way, and then a waiter appeared and it was time for dinner.

Levi gestured her ahead of him and Sophie pulled up short at the candlelit veranda; a glass ceiling showcased the glorious starlit sky above a table that glowed with white linen and silver cutlery. 'Amazing room.'

'Very civilised,' Levi agreed, as if he were still surprised by it. Even that offended her, as if they couldn't put on a good show up here in the bush.

She took her seat and, much to Sophie's amazement, dinner proved a delightful affair. They were joined by the resort manager, Steve, a handsome young man— more Odette's age than Levi's—who said and did all the right things and was very anxious to ensure that Odette was safely seated or served, as if she were an invalid. Baby phobia, Sophie guessed, but he left Sophie with a feeling of awkwardness she couldn't explain.

The rapport between Levi and Odette showed genuine affection. Reluctantly Sophie admitted she liked that—family was important—so he had some redeeming features which she didn't really want to see. And Levi devoted himself to being a wonderful host. Then again, her ex, Brad, had been a great host too.

Odette remained animated and 'William' held his own end of the conversation up for a change. Sophie had to shut her mouth when she would normally have answered for her brother until finally she subsided in awe at his previously hidden ability to socialise. He could have come on his own after all. Great!

Until the talk turned to helicopters and the suggestion of a joint expedition the next day. This she couldn't keep silent on. 'I hope you don't expect me to go along. Helicopters fall out of the sky.'

Levi sat back in his chair and smiled at her. 'No, they don't.'

Loosened up by the delightful Margaret River Shiraz, Sophie pointed her finger at him. 'I want to know what happens when the engine stops in a helicopter.'

Her comment came in a lull and stilled the other conversations, and Levi tilted his head at her. 'They glide. Autorotation. Instead of the air being pulled in from the top by the engine, the rotors turn the other way and pull the air in from underneath as you descend. Gives you fairly good forward and downward control. Like a winged aeroplane, just not as far.'

She didn't believe him. 'How far?'

'Enough to get passengers on the ground without hurting them.' He held her gaze, daring her to disbelieve him.

Sounded too simple. 'Then you can take off again?'

He rubbed his chin. 'Maybe not always without hurting the chopper.' He seemed sure of his facts.

Sophie digested that.

'We've two helicopters at Xanadu,' Steve said, 'and never had a problem.' He smiled kindly at her and she almost felt patted like a small dog. Sophie wondered why she had the urge to wipe the smile off his face. Maybe the poor guy had trained himself to be extra accommodating around his VIP guests, but Sophie found his attentions irritating.

She glanced at Levi but she couldn't read anything in his face. He was probably used to people fawning over him.

The conversation moved on and Sophie sat back to observe. She watched mostly Levi, despite her attempts not to be drawn to him. He made no blatant attempt to direct the conversation, he just did. While she didn't like him she had to admit he was smooth. He seemed to know the right thing to bring out the passion in Smiley for the land, and Sophie was surprised by her brother's apparent liking for their host.

Sophie refused to fall for the same thing and she wasn't going to lose. Actually, she wanted to go home or at least get out of this room, away from him.

With the meal cleared away, Sophie drifted towards the end of the veranda where the steps led down to the path around the side of the homestead. The stars winked down at her and the further she moved away from the veranda the brighter the sky lights formed into the constellations and patterns she'd grown up with.

The Southern Cross, the Pot, the Milky Way. A wooden bench under a huge boab looked the perfect place to hide. She sank gratefully down on warm wood in the dimness, and the soft breeze rattled the boab leaves over her head as if to soothe her.

Until Levi strode out onto the veranda with his satellite phone and shattered the magic of the night, along with the calm she'd achieved.

Typical city man. They never stopped. No doubt he couldn't imagine being without a phone at his fingertips, to direct underlings and ensure nobody forgot how important he was, and to order up the next convenience. Or like Brad, to check that his woman was waiting patiently at home, while he dallied somewhere else.

She'd like to see Levi bogged in a bulldust hole with no handy phone. See how resourceful he'd be with nobody but himself to rely on.

Then he saw her, ended the conversation and snapped his phone shut. She leant back into the shadows in a futile move as if he would forget she was there, slightly guilty about her mean thoughts for a man she barely knew, but still bitter by personal experience from the callousness of a man like him.

He paused at the bottom of the steps, and she thought he probably didn't even want to get his shoes dirty out here. Her nose wrinkled.

Levi hesitated at the bottom step, quite sure Sophie didn't want company, and reluctant to force his company on her. 'Coffee is ready if you'd like some.' He glanced at the grass. 'Unless you'd prefer it out here?'

She stood and walked towards him with a swish of her blue dress and he felt the rebuke for ruining her peace. She had attitude all right, he thought, but she carried it well. 'Thank you. Inside will be fine.'

There was no doubt the less she saw of him, the better, and no doubt either that the less he saw of her, the better.

CHAPTER THREE

LEVI stopped as he entered the room for breakfast on the veranda next morning. It seemed he'd interrupted an amusing show.

His sister, with much eye batting and smiles, was trying to convince cowboy William to do the scenic tourist fly in the chopper. Apparently they should fly to the Bungle Bungles, a massive prehistoric range of striped domes at the edge of the Tanami Desert, with a picnic basket, an idea which left a horrified expression on Sophie the orchid's face. Intriguing situation.

He could see a ride in the helicopter was the last thing Sophie wanted to do, make that second last. If he read her expression right when she glanced at him, the last thing she wanted was to stay behind at Xanadu, alone, with him.

Levi could tell. That was amusing too. Sort of. Though he'd never had someone blatantly avoid his company before.

He sat down next to Sophie at breakfast, maybe too

deliberately close, so his thigh touched hers when he turned, and he could actually feel her thrum with awareness. The fresh herby stuff she'd washed her hair with teased his nose and some psycho inside wanted to sniff her head. Now that would go over well as a space invasion.

Even her skin glowed golden in the morning light, like the honey on the crumpet she nibbled at, and reminded him he'd spent more than a few hours in bed last night trying not to remember those lush little hips and lips. He must be having a crisis.

'Good morning, Sophie.'

'Morning.' Her answer was accompanied by a darting look that came and went as she shrank her shoulders to avoid contact.

He had to bite back a smile. Becoming a habit those smiles. Very strange. 'Did you sleep well?'

'Fine, thanks.' Another flick of her eyes and he relented and shifted his chair a few inches away to give her some space. Her delightful shoulders actually sank with relief and he wondered why he was playing with her. He wasn't normally pushy.

'Did you sleep?' It seemed she could talk easier too.

Now how reluctantly had she asked that? He bit his lip. 'No, not really. The symphony of the night seemed especially loud.'

She raised those stern brows of hers. 'Kept awake by nature? Poor you. Well, it is a wilderness park.' She tossed her head. 'Sure beats the heck out of traffic noise.'

Maybe she didn't need sympathy. She could stand up for herself. So they ate their meal in silence as Odette continued to flirt with William.

Levi rubbed his chin as they all stood to leave because, funnily enough, her lack of enthusiasm for the flight made his skin itch.

'Odette?' he said, and his sister turned back.

'Look after Sophie. Remember, she's not comfortable, so no stunts.'

Odette raised her eyebrows at him and saluted. 'Yes, sir.'

Sophie sent him a semi-grateful look over her shoulder as she dragged her feet to follow the other two to the helipad.

Levi frowned to himself as he went the other way. He needed to concentrate on the paperwork he had to get through before they returned to Sydney, but the ridiculously blue Kimberley sky outside the window invited sacrifice. Odette was too pregnant to be pilot. And Sophie looked unhappy.

Unhappy was too mild a word. Sophie didn't know how she'd agreed to this.

Now Steve, the resort manager, had shooed Odette away from pre-flight checks. 'I can't let a pregnant lady do that,' he said with that tilted smile that prickled right up Sophie's nose. There was something about him that reminded her of someone but she couldn't connect the impression.

She'd never had much to do with the people from

Xanadu and apparently he'd been here for a few years and very close to the late owner. She wished he'd mind his own business though.

To make matters worse, just before take-off, Levi appeared and decreed he'd pilot instead of Odette. Suddenly Sophie could have stayed behind. Talk about bad luck.

Everyone was looking out for Odette. Which was a good thing, but Sophie wondered if it was too late to look out for herself. Now the new seating arrangements meant she'd be up front next to Levi. This kept getting better and better. Not.

The front helicopter seat was as bad as she'd imagined. She shrank back into the stiff leather, semi-frozen, not quite believing she'd agreed to this, when Levi reached in from the outside to click her belt into place. His hands pulled the belt firmly across her and snapped it shut. Talk about space invasion. This whole expedition was crazy and way out of her comfort zone. How the heck had she found herself next to him in a doorless chopper with only the seat belt between her and certain death?

And on that note, surely there should have been more seat belts or harnesses or something? One belt didn't seem enough.

Odette and Smiley chatted happily, ensconced in the rear out of sight and out of earshot. Once they got going, she thought bitterly, they'd be safe in their own little world.

Levi climbed in and she squashed herself back against the seat. He pointed to the bulky headphones hooked on the central support in front of her, and indicated she put them on.

'Can you hear me?' His metallic voice made her jump, and she looked across at him and glared. He nodded and she nodded facetiously back. He frowned, then went on. 'It's automatically switched to receive, so for you to be heard by everyone else just press this button to speak.'

He withdrew his attention from her and glanced in the back. 'You guys all buckled up?'

Odette's voice crackled. 'Roger.'

Levi glanced around the deserted helipad and began the pre-flight sequence. 'All clear,' he said to no one in particular and started the rotors.

The next few minutes Sophie missed as her eyes were tightly shut. The distant noise through the headphones grew louder and she felt the shudder from the flimsy craft right through the backs of her knees, then the first sideways swish of movement through the air and then back the other way.

She opened one eye. It was too hard not to look. They swayed a little from side to side as they edged higher and she could see the downdraught from the rotors beating the bushes below.

Then she could see the river at the bottom of the gorge, the roof of the homestead, the tops of the trees, and it was all a little intriguing, though she still pushed herself deep into her seat. She tried to relax her shoulders but the fear she'd fall out kept her rigid in the chair.

They climbed higher, and despite the lack of doors, she was protected from the wind by the bubble of the front windshield, and actually it didn't feel too bad.

She opened the other eye. There was a Perspex floor in front of her feet. What sort of sick person designed a helicopter with a see-through floor? If she'd had eyes in the bottom of her soles she'd be able to look through the Perspex to the ground.

Basically she was standing on a thin edge above certain death. Her eyes closed at the vertigo of that thought, then opened again to risk a glance towards Levi as he concentrated on the dials at the front of the cockpit. What was he looking at? Was everything OK? She studied the instrument panel herself for something familiar. Maybe she'd even find a reassuring needle. Shame the guy wasn't more into smiling but at least he was taking the danger of the situation seriously.

Knots—they were doing eighty knots, and that was faster than miles per hour, so fairly fast. Fuel—there were seventy gallons of fuel; tank was full anyway. Guess that meant if they crashed she'd die in a ball of flame.

She looked away. Maybe don't read the dials. They'd climbed higher while she'd been contemplating the manner of their deaths, and she could look down on the escarpment now.

This was pretty amazing. And when she looked back, carefully, towards the homestead and the serpentine river, it made her appreciate how remote the properties were out here.

She'd flown on jets from Perth to Kununurra but they'd been much higher and she'd never really noticed individual stations, though mostly because she'd chosen the aisle seat and not the window.

'We'll fly up and over the waterfall on the property.' Levi's voice crackled through the headphones. 'Odette likes that and then over to Lake Argyle. We'll pass over a couple of stations William asked to see, then in over the Bungles and back out over the Kimberley diamond mine and home.'

He was telling her this because…? Her stomach sank. She pushed the button to speak. 'Sounds like a long flight. Do we land anywhere?'

His teeth flashed. He couldn't possibly be concentrating enough on his job if he could smile about it, she thought sourly. 'Anywhere you want,' he said.

She resisted saying, *Here*, but not by much, and just nodded and turned away to glance at her watch. They'd be home in a few hours. She hoped.

Actually, the next hour passed fairly quickly. The waterfall looked surreal from above with sparkling drops at the side of the main body of water shimmering on the breeze to the gorge below.

Lake Argyle loomed indigo blue and stretched for ever, apparently seven times the size of Sydney Harbour, so that must be why it seemed to take seven times longer than she expected to cross.

When they flew over the isolation of the two cattle stations, Smiley asked Levi to circle again, so he could point out how they corralled their cattle using the land formations to form a natural bottleneck and arena. These were the stations Smiley had his eye on.

Sophie tried to concentrate on the implications of a station with no contact with the world for at least four months during the wet season, but all she could feel were the g-forces pulling her towards the open doorway. Her whole body seemed to be straining against the seat belt as they circled, and she had this horrible feeling that maybe Levi hadn't fastened her buckle properly and she'd just pop out of it into spiralling space.

Now that was a dilemma. She hadn't checked the belt herself but if she touched it now she might press the eject button.

Come on. Their aircraft was circling thousands of feet above the hard earth and Smiley was going on about the logistical difficulties of cattle to market.

It was no good. 'Can we land soon?' Sophie's voice cut across Smiley's, squeaky with distress, and she felt Levi glance at her.

The helicopter levelled out. 'Bungles in fifteen minutes, you right with that?' Levi's voice was still tinny, but the strange thing was the lack of humour, just genuine understanding and concern in his voice and the reassurance she gained from that. His hand came across and rested on her upper arm as if to transfer calmness. From a man she didn't trust it shouldn't have helped that much. But it did. Like a lifeline.

Funny how she'd never felt that mixture of empathy and support from Brad's touch and she'd been engaged to him.

Inexplicably steadied, she nodded, and allowed herself to sag more into the seat and close her eyes. Think calm thoughts. Take deep breaths. Everything will be fine.

That was when the engine spluttered, coughed and died. Her eyes flew open. Slow motion from that moment on.

Suddenly there was no background noise except the wind and the rotors turning without an engine. She watched in horror as Levi kept his hands glued to the controls, correcting the cabin's inclination to yaw. Levi's voice travelled down the tunnel of her frozen mind. 'Have to land fast.' His voice was much louder without the sound of the engine, then she couldn't hear him at all because he'd switched the radio from the cabin to transmit the distress call. But she could watch his lips move, grimly, as he enunciated their position.

Unwilling to stare frozenly out of the Perspex beneath her feet she kept her eyes on Levi.

Glide. Helicopters can glide like planes but not as far. She remembered him saying that. She believed him. But he did lie. Had he lied then too? Surely not about this?

They weren't falling like a stone at the moment, still going forward, but the altimeter was unwinding like a top, much, much faster than it had wound up. Then she remembered that Odette and Smiley were in the back but she couldn't turn her neck to look. They'd all die. Odette's baby too? No. They had to survive. That thought steadied her. She was the midwife. The only medical person. They'd need her. Odette's baby needed her. She'd better survive in one piece.

She stared at Levi, who looked as if his face was hewn from the same stone as the escarpment they hurtled towards as he wrestled with the controls. No panic, just fierce, implacable determination to win. Thank God he'd decided to be the pilot. Even now he inspired confidence.

Then there was no time for thoughts. Just the sickening rush of the ground towards them, and she tucked her chin onto her chest and hugged her knees, so she must have listened to all those hostesses on flights she'd tried to block out. Thank you, hostesses.

They were coming in too fast.

The impact flung her head back as the helicopter slammed into the ground. Someone screamed and she wasn't sure if it was Odette or herself, then they clipped a boulder and the cabin flipped up and tipped sideways and landed once more with a larger crash and, finally, with agonising slowness, tipped back to settle on its base with a rattle of rocks and debris. They'd stopped. Intact.

That first few seconds of cessation of movement was more frightening than the seconds before, where at least she'd known she was alive. She straightened her aching neck to look at Levi. He didn't move; his long lashes were resting on ashen cheeks, and for a horrific moment she thought he was dead. Then she saw the rise and fall of his chest and the relief made the nausea rise in her throat. She reached across for his hand that lay limply pointed at her and felt for his pulse. It was fast but steady and she heaved a sigh of relief.

A soft moan came from behind her and, gingerly, she turned her head. 'Odette? Smiley? You both all right?'

'I think William's unconscious. What about Levi?'

'His pulse is strong but he's out too. We hit some scrub on their side of the aircraft so I think they bore the brunt of it.' She didn't know whether to ask or not. 'Your baby? Everything all right there?'

'I think so.' Odette's voice cracked. 'We need to get out. Get them out. The fuel!'

Sophie's fingers grappled with her belt clasp. The locking mechanism wouldn't open and those ball-of-flame visions returned to add desperation to her frustration. She rattled the catch.

Levi's hand came across and pushed the release and suddenly she was free. 'It's OK. I'll do it.' Why was he whispering?

He was conscious. Thank God. 'You were knocked out.'

'Hmm,' he said, his voice still weak, and rubbed the

front of his head. Then he blinked and sat up straighter.
'You OK? Out!' He turned his attention to the back seat
but Odette was already on the ground and attempting
to rouse Smiley.

Sophie scrambled up from her seat and climbed over
the scattered wreckage at the front of the craft to help
Odette. Smiley groaned but didn't open his eyes and
Sophie lifted his lids to peer into his eyes. His pupils
contracted with the light and she heaved a sigh of relief.
No time for sympathy. 'Wake up, Smiley. Move!'

Smiley's eyelids fluttered and he groaned. 'What
happened?'

Levi was out and beside them now too. He swayed
ever so slightly and Sophie watched him with narrowed
eyes. 'Later, sport,' Levi said. 'Let's get you out of
here, though I think if the tank was going to explode it
would have done before now.' He shooed both women
with his hand. 'Get away, over by those trees, you two.
Now.'

Odette turned and hobbled away but Sophie stood
her ground. 'Maybe he shouldn't be moved.'

'No choice.' Levi frowned at Smiley. 'Can you move
your fingers and toes?'

'My leg hurts.'

'No tingling?' Smiley shook his head, then grimaced, and tried to pull himself free but recoiled his
arm back to his chest with a loud groan.

The hiss of liquid hitting hot metal made them all
jump. Levi frowned. 'I'll do the work, just brace your

arm.' He heaved Smiley sideways and onto the ground in one huge movement and then dragged him away from the aircraft with Sophie almost glued to his back. The intermittent hiss from behind hastened their steps.

Sophie looked back over her shoulder. 'I'm glad it only just started doing that.'

Levi propped Smiley against a tree. 'I could have lived without it. We'll give it some time to cool down and then see what's happening with the radio, as long as everyone is stable.'

He turned to his sister, who hovered over Smiley. 'What about you, Odette? Your baby?'

'I'm not hurt. He's moving normally. Is William all right?'

'Fine. I'm more worried about you.' He looked at Sophie, who nodded and drew his sister to a fallen tree to sit.

'You need to sit for a while, Odette. We've fallen out of the sky.' She shook her head. Holy dooley. 'We're alive but it's crazily worse than a car accident and babies don't like being in those. You sure you're not contracting?'

Odette stroked her belly. 'It doesn't hurt.'

'OK. But sit. While I check Smiley.'

'His name is William,' Odette said. 'Smiley sounds like a dummy and he's not that.'

Sophie blinked. Good grief. That's all she needed. 'William,' she said but rolled her eyes as she turned away.

CHAPTER FOUR

Levi glowered at the wreckage of the aircraft and shook his head as they all gathered their breath. 'An engine should never do that.' His jaw clamped tight and she could see the implacable leader who highly resented mechanical failure.

Well, yes. She wasn't too impressed about it herself but even she knew the unexpected was possible.

Nobody else said anything and Sophie asked the question. 'What happened?'

Levi ignored her and turned to his sister. 'You saw nothing out of order in the pre-flight check, Odette?'

His sister grimaced. 'I only started it—Steve finished it.'

Levi's face stilled. 'It's not your fault.' He spoke very quietly, and Sophie frowned as she tried to gather the thread of undertones and make sense of it, but for some reason the hairs on her arms prickled and stood and she lifted her arms across her chest to rub them.

Levi was muttering. 'I can't believe I didn't do my

own pre-flight check as well. You should never do anything last minute when flying. No excuses. First rule of flight.'

He glanced at the sky. 'We're baking in the sun. We need more shade and definitely water. I'll go up the gorge to see if there's a creek or a pool.'

Levi to the rescue? She didn't think so. 'Let me. As soon as I've checked—' she glanced at Odette and corrected herself '—William.'

Levi looked pale; a purple bruise had begun on his temple, and she could see him blaming himself when he'd saved them all. Sophie went on. 'You've been knocked out. You should move to the shade and I'll find the water.' She'd avoided his eyes while she spoke and flicked a glance back to see how he took her suggestion. Not well, judging by the scowl he directed at her.

He straightened, until he loomed over her, but the effect was spoilt when he swayed slightly. 'Who died and elected you captain? I can make my own decisions. Thanks.'

Sophie shrugged. He didn't intimidate her. Grumpy sod. 'It's a small job. As I'm the only medical person and you look like death warmed up, I say you need to rest after your heroics earlier. You're still the captain, just concussed, so that's what you'll do.'

He blinked, didn't quite drop his mouth open, but she knew she'd surprised him. He looked about to say something but didn't and she glanced at Odette and lowered her voice. 'Someone needs to keep an eye on your sister and give me a yell if she complains of any pain too, though I won't be long.'

She looked at her brother. 'But Smiley first.'

Levi hovered while she examined Smiley and it was hard to ignore him. She'd have liked to tell him to sit again but didn't want to push her luck. She doubted anyone had tried to tell him what to do since he was in school. It would do him good. Actually, thinking of him as a scrubby school boy did a lot for her confidence.

She spoke to Smiley. 'How's the head?' She ran her fingers lightly over the swelling under his right eye and then palpated the bulge over his ear. 'You've given it a good whack. Close your eyes for a couple of seconds and then open them.'

He did so and she watched his pupils constrict at the light. They looked equal as much as she could tell.

She checked his ears for discharge but there was none, and it made her think she should do the same for Levi. She looked at him.

'My ears are fine,' he said quickly. 'And I'm sure my pupils are too.'

Sophie shrugged. 'Your choice,' she said, not eager for another clash of wills, and looked back at Smiley.

'So you've dislocated the shoulder again?' A sister's tone.

Smiley grimaced. 'I'd say.'

'We can fix that. We've done it before.' But she really didn't want to think about doing that. 'And the ankle?'

'Pretty sore.' They all looked at it, swollen already, and she ran her hands over it but couldn't feel any blatant deviations of line.

Poor Smiley. 'That's gotta hurt. We'll splint it, get you a walking stick and at least you'll be independent for short walks. You still wear your knife?'

He nodded and patted his hip with his good hand. 'Good,' she said, and looked at him with sympathy for the impending pain. 'You want to do the shoulder now before it swells more?'

Tight-lipped but still brief. 'Quicker the better.'

Sophie looked at Levi. 'Can you help me with this?'

Levi appeared even more dubious. 'You sure you know what you're doing?'

Did he think she did this stuff for fun? 'I've done it for Smiley twice before.' And hated it.

Levi opened his mouth and then closed it again. 'If he's got faith in you, then I'm happy to help. Just tell me what you want me to do.' Deferring to her? Not what he'd said a minute ago but she didn't think it a good time to point that out.

He still looked uncomfortable and she wondered if he was feeling faint again. 'You sure you're OK, Levi?'

'I'm fine.' The terse man was back. He looked at Smiley. 'What about his pain relief.'

She shook her head. 'The sooner I line the bones up again so they'll slide back in, the better. And he's been knocked out anyway. Not a good idea.'

Sophie took a deep breath and hoped everyone

couldn't see how sick this made her. She knelt down beside Smiley and cleared the dirt in front of him of rocks and sticks for him to lie down.

She'd need a piece of material to go around Smiley's chest and under his injured armpit that Levi could pull on while she manipulated Smiley's arm. It needed to be strong like clothing. Probably her blouse would be best. Actually, it could be Levi's shirt. She thought about that and decided she didn't want to see his chest. She had a fair idea of the picture that might lodge in her brain.

'We'll use my shirt.' She turned around before any-one could say anything and slipped it off. Businesslike, as if she wasn't really sitting there in front of them all in her lacy bra, and she refused to think about whether she had little rolls of belly as she bent over. This day just kept getting better and better.

She spread her shirt on the ground to roll the material up in a long sausage and slipped it around Smiley's body and under his armpit until the two ends met back on Levi's side.

'Down you go, Smiley. Shuffle forward so you can stretch out on your back.' Smiley eased down with agonised slowness. She looked at Levi. 'Just kneel down facing him on the uninjured side and hold the ends firmly like handles.'

Levi knelt beside Smiley and concentrated on the task as he gathered the ends. He should be doing this, not her, but it didn't seem the right moment to pull rank on her. It had been a lot of years since he'd done any generalist work like dislocations. He'd bet she'd be wild when she found out.

She was directing them like an annoying but perky little conductor in her bra and shorts and he liked her more than when she'd been sexily annoying in her blue dress. Because she was bending towards Smiley her breasts were falling his way. In a gesture of respect he faded out her cleavage, which was no mean feat, and watched her hands.

She surprised him with her calmness and methodical approach to something he could probably have done but not as confidently as she was. Qualifications meant zip against recent experience, he reassured himself.

Sophie nodded. 'Keep both ends together under his good armpit. When I take his other arm you keep the pressure on his chest so he can't follow me.'

Levi could hear his sister mumbling behind him as she agonised over William's impending discomfort. He wished she'd be quiet.

Sophie must have heard her too. 'He'll be fine, Odette. I know we're all still shell-shocked from the crash but he'll be OK.' Sophie looked his way. 'As long as Levi doesn't tickle him, 'cause it hurts to laugh.'

Levi blinked in surprise at her comment and compressed his lips to bite back the smile. Effective stress relief. She was a tough little cookie, though he'd begun to wonder if she really was as tough as she made out, because he could detect a tiny tremor in her hands every now and then. 'Nurses have a dreadful sense of humour, eh, William?'

Smiley had his eyes shut. 'Hmm.'

But the tension had lessened a little and even Odette got the hint to relax. He watched Sophie's face as she concentrated. Something made him want to reach out and touch her arm, just for support, like he had during the flight when he realized she'd started to panic, but he didn't want to interrupt her thoughts. It was almost as if she was rehearsing the steps.

He was right. She was. Sophie knelt down and after a brief stroke of sympathy she took her brother's elbow and gently bent it so that his fingers pointed to the sky they'd just fallen out of. She didn't even want to think about sky-falling. Bend arm at ninety-degree angle from his body, Sophie recited to herself.

'Keep the pressure on now,' she said quietly to Levi, and began to pull, still gently but firmly, on the bent elbow, away from Smiley's body. Then she rotated the arm on the shoulder joint as if Smiley was trying to throw a baseball.

Sweat beaded on Smiley's forehead as she moved it slowly back and forward until the shoulder slid back into place with a click that made everyone wince.

'OK.' Now Sophie felt like crying or heaving or running away but she couldn't do any of those things. 'We need a sling.'

She looked at Smiley and he gave her a small wink. 'Thanks, Sis.'

'Don't do it again. You know I hate it.' She dropped a kiss on his forehead and Levi was there to help her stand. She hadn't even noticed he'd moved, and secretly she was glad of his support because her legs wobbled.

His hand kept hold of hers and he pulled her gently into his chest for a moment in a purely asexual embrace, though his shirt against her nose meant she could only inhale air laced with Levi. His arms rested around her back, firmly but not cloying, just for that moment so she could rest her head on him and close her eyes and regroup. Strangely, the hug wasn't an invasion of space as much as a recoup of resources and exactly what she needed.

She stepped back and his arms fell. 'Thanks. I hate doing that for him.' She flabbergasted herself with the honesty and he looked just as surprised as she did. Normally she wouldn't let anyone know when she felt overwhelmed. She prided herself on self-sufficiency and she would have thought Levi was the last person she'd want to tell about any weakness on her end. It had to be part of the shock.

She watched his hands flick the dirt from her shirt and smooth it, and he even held it out for her to slip her arms in. She felt strangely cosseted but weepy. Not something she was used to at all. And she wasn't even sure she liked the feeling. 'Well done, Sophie,' he said quietly. She couldn't meet his eyes in case he saw the glitter.

She looked at her shirt in his hands. 'Umm. I need to tear a bit off the bottom to make a sling.'

He shook his head. 'Put it on. Mine's bigger. You don't want to get a sunburnt strip around your waist.'

She took it and turned away to collect herself. A hug was OK but sympathy when she was emotional was such a pain. She sniffed unobtrusively. Men were so good at that. Twisting the knife when you were trying to gain control. She heard the rip of his shirt as he made the sling and she kept her eyes averted. She took a couple of deep breaths and turned back to face the group.

To her surprise Levi had achieved a very creditable sling. 'Distinction in a first-aid course, eh?' she said in a poor attempt of a joke. She saw the look from Odette to Levi and Levi's shake of the head but Sophie was too mentally exhausted to go there.

'Something like that.' He looked at Smiley. 'So how's the shoulder now?'

'Good as new.' They all knew it'd still be painful.

Levi gave him a crooked smile. 'I'll bet.' He glanced at Sophie. 'I can do splints and bandages but we'll do that after you check we have a water supply.'

'Yes, Captain.' She couldn't resist. 'Next time we come into land here I'll try to have a look as we approach.'

'Good idea.' He stood. 'There's a couple of water bottles in the chopper. I'll get them and check the radio if it's all cooled down a bit.' He rubbed his chin.

'Though I think I'll come with you, after I discuss something with Odette.'

Sophie sighed. He was determined, then. His funeral. She had to stop saying that. It was obviously a bad omen.

Levi hadn't been keen for her to hang around the wreck so she wandered slowly towards the gully, pleased to have a moment before he joined her.

The chance to walk away from the crash site was welcome and she dawdled along the gorge, watching the ground for signs of animals. She didn't hear him come up beside her and she jumped when he spoke.

'So you think we'll find water?'

She glanced at him. 'Pretty confident.'

'Fine,' he said, but raised his brow sceptically.

She frowned. 'The wet season's not long finished, and rock pools and depressions in the gorge floor should still hold water.' She should know. She'd walked so many gorges in her lifetime apparently preparing for just such an occasion.

Hopefully, the water wouldn't be too old either, but there'd be enough to keep them until help arrived. Which shouldn't be long if the distress call went through.

As they walked, long grey-green grasses poked out at them, and as they brushed past Sophie inhaled the warm air and everything felt brighter and cleaner—and even more precious for nearly being snatched away.

'I can't believe how close we've came to crashing

badly.' It was very queer how Levi in command had lessened the horror. That they'd all managed to escape fairly unscathed so far—and that even Odette's baby hadn't been fazed by their rough landing—was a miracle assisted by Levi's determination they would survive.

Levi didn't say anything and she wondered if he'd always been this taciturn. He needed to smell the roses. They were alive!

'See how the cliffs beside us soar into the bluest sky. Don't the walls look like red-brick? It reminds you of millions of years in creation and some of the oldest dated rocks in the world, doesn't it?'

'No, Pollyanna. It reminds me we've had to force land in the middle of nowhere with very little to keep us alive.'

She frowned at him. 'Lighten up. The Aboriginal people survived.' Sophie spread her arms. 'You'll see in the overhangs and caves they'll have left their stories for us on the rock. They've been a part of this land for thousands of years. We'll manage a day or two.'

'Spare me from eternal optimism.'

'And me from a grump.'

She was only a hundred metres from the plane when she found the break in the range she was looking for. They looked back before they turned into a narrow gorge off the main escarpment but Odette and Smiley were still sitting on the boulders they'd left them on.

It was cool in the gully, the sun not yet directly overhead to shine onto the narrow strip of valley floor.

'It would be worthwhile moving the others here to get out of the sun,' she commented. 'Especially if we have to wait long for rescue.'

'I'd been just about to suggest that. You beat me to it.'

She slanted an amused glance at him. 'I'm annoying you, then?'

'Not at all.'

Liar, she thought. Tufts of sharp spinifex scratched at her ankles as she scrambled over boulders that had tumbled down from the walls, and Levi followed her. Within only a few minutes she'd come upon the first pool and she raised her brows at him. See!

'OK,' he said. 'It's water. Looks a bit green.'

'It's just starting to algae, but the middle of the pool will be clear and no doubt cold.' He didn't look convinced. 'It's a good time of the year if you have to crash,' she teased him. 'Those tiny fish don't know their pond'll disappear over the next few months.'

'I guess fish prove the water's clean enough to drink.'

'Yep. In fact, the traditional owners use bunches of sharp spinifex to brush the pools and capture the tiny fish in the barbs. Then they burn it and eat the fish. We might try that later.' She crouched at the edge to fill her bottle, peripherally aware of the snake trail to her left. The smooth indent in the fine gravel was a timely reminder to watch for basking reptiles. She had a feeling he wasn't ready to know that yet.

Levi couldn't believe this woman. She talked as if

they were filming for a nature show, not about their survival in one of the most remote places in the world.

She sat back and glanced around as she screwed the lid back on the water bottle, then washed her hands before bathing her face and lower arms. His eyes were drawn to the way she slid the water over the inside of her wrists and then lifted her fingers to allow the trickles to run down her neck and beneath the collar of her blouse.

Hastily he leaned forward and rinsed his own hands. It was cold all right, just what he needed after the heat on the valley floor. Not to mention the other heat.

'So we have water, and a few tiny fish to eat. Our own bush-tucker chef. It could be worse.' He wasn't sure how.

'We're alive.'

He nodded soberly. True. All of them, and that was a miracle. No thanks to the person who'd tampered with the aircraft and the concept still had the power to make him wild enough to want to crush a rock with his bare hands.

She must have noticed his frown because she flicked a tiny drop of water at him. 'Don't suppose you fancy a witchetty grub. Apparently they taste like eggs. I can see a witchetty tree and I could dig the roots up for you.'

He had to smile. Retribution could wait. 'Pass.'

When they returned to the crash site the full extent of their miracle of survival again made itself very plain. Sophie stood for a moment and shook her head and

Levi silently agreed. Pieces of the helicopter were strewn from where they first skidded down past the wreck, and the cabin itself looked more like a drink can that had been beaten by a stick than a mode of travel.

The others had moved a few feet back against the canyon wall out of the sun and sat on boulders that had fallen from the cliffs. 'You'd have to be unlucky, but I'm not sure I'd feel real comfortable waiting for another boulder to fall where they're sitting.'

Levi nodded. 'We'll move to the gorge as soon as I empty the aircraft.'

They separated, he to the aircraft and she to Odette.

CHAPTER FIVE

LEVI spread the first-aid kit and the tool box out on the ground to see what was available, and he looked up as Sophie laughed out loud at something Odette had said. At least someone could laugh about the situation they were in. His eyes were drawn to her when she stood and approached his work area.

Her white shirt was dusty and her disarranged hair looked not unlike the spinifex tufting the bottom of the canyon. Actually, she looked pretty fantastic, considering she'd had her worst nightmare confirmed by a crash landing. He'd been mulling over her behaviour since the crash while he worked and he'd come to the conclusion he'd never met a woman like her.

Her composure when she'd reduced her brother's shoulder still impressed him. She'd done a better job than he would have. It was far too long since he'd done any emergency work apart from eyes and he was glad he hadn't had to practise on Smiley.

His lack of disclosure about his medical background

had become an elephant he could've done without, but it didn't seem the right moment to correct the impression he'd given. Hopefully, when he did, she'd just laugh it off, though it was unlikely, if the first conversation they'd had at Xanadu was anything to go by. The longer he left it, the bigger the elephant grew, but he really didn't have the capacity to take on a discussion of his work.

Still, she looked pretty pleased with herself and it was a bonus to find something to smile about after what he'd just discovered. 'Odette feels better?' Levi said.

'Yep. And Smiley's fine.'

'That's great.' He paused. 'Do you want the good news or the bad news?'

Her smile died and he regretted that, but he wasn't joking. 'Can I have bad and then good to cheer me up?' she asked reluctantly.

'The bad news is the radio's dead.'

'That's really bad.' Her face fell further. 'And the good news?'

'The good news is the aircraft wouldn't have gone up in flames because the fuel tank was on Empty.'

He watched her think about that until finally she said, 'Then what was the hissing?'

She had a logical mind, he'd give her that. 'The oil dripping on the hot engine.'

A tiny line crinkled between her brows. 'But how could the fuel be on Empty? I saw it at Full on the gauge.'

He had an idea but it wasn't a very nice one. 'Must have sprung a leak.'

The crinkle deepened, and actually she looked cute, but it sure wasn't the time to notice that. 'Do fuel tanks do that?'

Never in his lifetime. He sighed. 'Not usually.'

He watched her shake her head—a lot of that head shaking had been going on around here—and he wished he didn't have to explain the rest. He gave her a minute to mull it over and looked at the minimal supplies they had to survive on. Not much there, which was what he'd had a quick word to Odette about before he'd left with Sophie.

'You say the radio's dead. Why is that dead?'

He appreciated how calmly she'd taken his first news. Hysterics would have really done his head in. 'I'd like to know that too.' He saw the beginnings of comprehension as her eyes widened.

'So what are you saying? Didn't you talk to someone as we were landing? I saw your lips move.'

He remembered that moment. It hadn't been pleasant. 'I wish I could offer more reassurance but I can't. I didn't get a response so I gave the position in case they could hear me, even though I couldn't hear them. I don't know if it worked.'

She made a silent *O* with her mouth. Her face was like a book. No subterfuge. No doubt she'd scorn such a thing. She was so different from any woman he'd met and with such a well of strength that was almost scary.

Thank goodness he liked his women sweet and compliant.

By now, Odette and William had left their perch on the boulders to join the others.

'It was a good idea anyway,' Sophie said earnestly, as if sorry he felt bad. She made him smile. That was twice now. Then she said, 'But you've got one of those little GPS tracker things, don't you?'

'ELT. Emergency locator transmitter.' She didn't like what she saw on his face and he watched her transfer her attention to Odette for a more palatable answer.

Odette looked up. 'It seems someone took it out and didn't replace it,' Odette said baldly.

'Someone? Took it out?' Sophie actually squeaked, and suddenly he wanted to put his arm around her, but she backed away as if she knew what he was thinking. How could she know that?

She looked at her brother but all William did was shrug his good shoulder and not comment. Levi admired him for it. There wasn't much to say as the choices were limited. Someone had tried to kill them and nearly succeeded. None of the three of them mentioned the fact the chopper had been tampered with but it simmered there between them, except that Sophie, still focused on the radio not working, didn't get it. No bonus in her knowing.

Sophie sank down on a boulder and, as an afterthought, handed the water bottle again to Odette. She closed her eyes, sighed and visibly relaxed her shoulders. Finally she mumbled, 'Glad I'm not the captain,' opened her eyes and looked straight at him. 'What's the plan? Captain.'

'Now she defers,' he said, but he was inordinately glad of her support. He wasn't quite sure when it was she'd stopped being annoying. 'William says he knows this area from mustering and there's an Aboriginal community a day's walk away if we head north. I'm thinking William and Odette should stay here, and you and I walk out and get help.'

She chewed her lip and glanced around the desolate landscape. 'It's breaking the first rule. Leaving the site. We're not that far from the desert and the sun's a furnace in the sky until five.' She looked at the supplies. 'But there's not a lot to eat out here once we get through the picnic basket.'

'My thoughts exactly.'

She narrowed her eyes. 'If we give them today to send a search party staying put is a good thing.' She looked at his sister and Levi had to keep from shaking his head in disbelief. She seemed so calm about the whole thing. 'How do you feel about that, Odette?' she said. As if it was a mundane cancellation of an appointment.

He watched his sister struggle to match her composure and he wished, fruitlessly, he'd been more firm when she'd been so determined to leave Sydney with him.

Odette brushed the hair off her forehead. 'William

can't walk far and I'm not much better. As long as we have water and a bit of food we'll be fine for a day, I guess.'

Sophie nodded and he thanked God again he'd been stranded with sensible people. He wondered if all of the people who lived out here in the back of beyond were like Sophie and William.

Apart from the fact that maybe someone was trying to kill his sister and him—but that was unproven—the place was growing on him.

'So we leave tomorrow morning early, do you think?' Sophie said.

He almost smiled again. She couldn't help being bossy, though he suspected she'd push herself harder than anyone else. 'Sounds like a plan.'

She nodded and stood. 'What would you like me to do?'

He was right. 'We'll collect wood first for a signal fire, then some for the camp tonight.'

'Sure.' Sophie stopped beside Odette again. 'No pains?' He could almost see the priorities ticking off in her mind.

Odette shook her head but her hand slid protectively over her stomach, as if to ward off the idea. William reached over with his good arm and caught her fingers and held them. Odette squeezed back.

'I'd hate to be the one who's pregnant,' William said.

Levi looked at Sophie. He'd been avoiding that horror. Unfortunately he knew the danger to his sister lay in the sudden deceleration of their landing. Forces that could tear an inelastic placenta off an elastic uterus. He'd seen that in the brief time he'd had in obstetrics, but there was nothing they could do at this moment except watch her.

Sophie crouched down, obviously thinking the same thing because she said, 'So how long since we crashed?'

'I thought it was a forced landing.' Levi pretended to be offended.

'I'm sorry,' she said over her shoulder as she faced Odette. 'How long is it since your incredible brother managed to avert disaster and get us to the ground safely, Odette?' There was humour in the words but none in her voice. She meant every word and he was surprised how they unexpectedly warmed the place that had iced over with the knowledge of foul play.

He'd never thought of himself as needy and he stamped the feeling out.

Odette looked at her watch. 'It feels like minutes but about an hour and a half?'

Sophie crouched and her hand hovered above Odette's uterus. 'May I?' She waited for permission, then rested her hand on the baby bulge. 'I'm thinking the first four hours are the most likely time you'd start contracting if there'd been any problems due to the landing. It's fabulous you haven't gone into labour already. But tell me if you get regular pains.'

Odette shook her head, as if by denying it, it wouldn't happen. 'Don't wish that on me.'

Sophie shook her head vehemently. 'I'm not, believe me. The longer it holds off the less likely your baby has any ill effects from the events.'

Odette chewed her lip as she stroked her belly. 'It's not quite the home birth I'd envisaged.'

Sophie rolled her eyes. 'It's not the day any of us envisaged, except maybe me when we took off.' She smiled ruefully. 'And I apologise if I brought us all bad luck.'

Not the person to blame. 'If it's someone's fault,' Levi said drily, 'it certainly wasn't yours.' He stood. 'I used to be a pretty mean Boy Scout so reckon I could manage a fire in case a plane flies over.'

'Then I'll start collecting wood as soon as we get to the gully.' Sophie looked around. 'So we'll need a campfire and a signal fire?'

Odette wiped her face. 'It's so hot. Hard to imagine we'll need heat.'

'It'll be cold tonight,' Smiley offered and squeezed Odette's hand. Poor Smiley. He'd hate being unable to help. Sophie was glad he was there for Odette. She'd the feeling if he hadn't been Odette would have succumbed to hysterics by now and that wouldn't have been fun. To give her due, she was a city girl and where they'd crashed was as far as she'd get from a city.

Odette scuffed at the dry grass beneath her feet. 'What if we start a bushfire?'

'As long as it blows the other way it's all good,' Smiley said, and spread the map one-handed that Levi had given him from the wreck.

He didn't enlarge so Sophie finished the sentence. 'In the Kimberleys bushfires are a way of life. We try to burn off the whole area every couple of years. Even as far out as here. The Aboriginal people have been burning off for thousands of years. For them it means the scrub stays sparse and they can see the animals they want to hunt. A lot of the trees and shrubs around here don't germinate until they've been through a fire. From our point of view, frequent fires germinate the land and prevent a massive fire that would be impossible to control.'

They packed up their meagre belongings and began walking towards the gully. Odette gazed around at, what was to her, desolate landscape. 'It's so sparse and different from anywhere I've ever been,' Odette said, as if they'd landed on the moon.

'William and I love it.' Sophie thought of Perth for the first time that day, only the second time since she'd seen Levi. Now that was queer. 'Perth's a pretty place— it has the ocean,' she said, trying to be fair but Brad lived there. 'I wouldn't live anywhere else than here though.' She looked at Levi as she spoke, and remembered that his appreciation of her land was confined to flying over it.

He raised his brows. 'Don't look at me like that. The Kimberleys are growing on me. Though you have great rivers and can't swim in them. And apparently it's the same in the ocean up here.'

'Maybe, but we have rock pools and gorges that are

fine. You just have to know where it's safe and where it's not. We're fine here from crocs, but watch the snakes as we walk.'

Levi glanced at his horrified sister and made a strangled sound but Sophie couldn't read anything in his face. Had he just laughed at her?

'I hate snakes.' Odette shuddered.

'If you see one just stop or back off real slowly. They panic too and are just as likely to run the same way as you and you'll think they're chasing you.'

'It won't be really chasing me. OK.' Odette shuddered again.

Levi was watching Sophie and she'd swear he was amused, even though his mouth didn't move. 'So you're a snake lover too?'

Sophie shook her head. 'It's their home too. Someone once told me that a snake has a really short memory, about forty seconds, which always makes me smile when I see one. I imagine them forgetting I'm there.'

After that conversation, when they moved up next to the mouth of the gully, Odette's head swivelled like one of those toy nodding dogs people used to sit on the back window of their cars. She walked with her brother, her hand tightly gripped to his arm.

Smiley leaned heavily on his stick with Sophie on his other side. 'I feel so bloody useless,' he said quietly.

'You're helping Odette which is great. She needs your calm. Will you manage when we go?'

Smiley looked around to ensure the others weren't in earshot. 'As long as she doesn't have the baby.'

Sophie whispered, 'It's just like a calf, Smiley, or a foal.'

He choked back a laugh. 'Great.' They grinned at each other. 'You'll run through a couple of things with me before you leave though?' he said. She nodded. She had to believe Odette wouldn't go into labour in the day they'd be away. It was too frightening a thought. Not that there was anything they could change.

Smiley examined the spot she'd chosen and nodded. 'At least up here I can get my own water.'

'It'll be tricky but you could.'

Levi came up to them with a long branch of dead wood he'd picked up on the way. 'We'll be out of the weather if one of the sudden tropical storms blows up.'

Everyone pitched in and there was a lip of overhang just past the entrance where they'd packed their supplies against the wall.

The afternoon passed as they watched for rescue, without reward, and prepared for the night. Back out in the main canyon they'd erected a signal fire with green leaves on top for smoke as a way to flag down a search plane if one flew over them, but the sky remained blue and clear of aircraft.

Technically they wouldn't be missed at Xanadu until almost nightfall. They'd told Steve they'd be back by late afternoon so they were not technically even missing yet.

Levi began to cut the long grass that Sophie suggested they use for beds for the night along the overhang, while she cleared the ground in front so they could make a fire to keep everyone warm. With the wall behind them the heat would be caught and the flames would keep any animals away.

At four o'clock they sat back and Sophie could see the activity had raised Odette's spirits. 'I'd say we're a clever bunch. We could make it on one of those television survivor shows.'

'Except there's no camera man with a satellite phone.' Odette looked at the depleted picnic basket. 'Who wants to go to the shop for a treat?'

Sophie spread her arms. 'There's plenty to eat around here.'

Levi dropped the last of the sticks for the night fire. 'Spare me from Pollyanna with bush tucker,' Levi said. 'Not witchetty grubs, I hope.'

Sophie refused to be downcast by the lack of enthusiasm. 'Must admit I've never been a fan of the old grub. Though they say ten grubs a day is enough for survival.' Levi didn't look convinced, so Sophie pushed on. 'And I did find a Gubinge tree up one of the gullies. I'll show you where, before dark, in case you want some tomorrow, Odette.' She held up the small greenish-yellow fruit which looked more like a pale pecan nut than a fruit. 'Known also as a Kakadu plum, it's easy to eat.'

Smiley sat quietly amused during her lecture and declined to sample the fruit. She frowned at him for not offering support but forgave him for the discomfort he was still in. No doubt he still felt sick and sore but he wasn't complaining. He never did. Actually, nobody was, so maybe she should revise her opinion a little about some city people.

She directed her attention to Levi and Odette and bit bravely into the skin. The tanginess twisted on her tongue and she fought to keep her face straight as she chewed and swallowed. 'Food for indigenous people for thousands of years and apparently has a hundred times more vitamin C than an orange.' She licked her lips and tried to define the taste. 'The juice crosses between a pear and an apple. There's a zing which I think is from the vitamin C but see what you think.' She tossed one each to Odette and Levi. 'Either way, it's the perfect refreshment if we're right out of grocery shops.'

'Bush tucker.' Levi looked at her from under his brows as if to say, *Are you having us on?* When she nodded encouragingly he bit into the fruit, and then finished it off. 'Not addictive, but not bad.'

Sophie nodded. 'We'll take some with us when we walk out.'

'Awesome.' He rubbed his hands together facetiously. So he did have a sense of humour. Now that was something Brad never had, and why she should think of Brad and Levi in the same minute sent a tiny flicker of fear into her belly which she was determined to ignore.

CHAPTER SIX

JUST before dawn the next morning, when the night birds were settling and the morning budgerigars shared their chatter, Levi and Sophie prepared to leave camp. The gentle breeze lifted the bumps on Sophie's arms and the ground crackled cold and hard beneath her socks. She tucked her chin into her collar as she pulled on her boots.

She glanced across to where Levi wore Smiley's broad Akubra and looked disturbingly like a country man rather than the city slicker she didn't trust. Much more dependable and much more dangerous to her peace of mind.

Sophie could smile at the image of her brother scowling uncomfortably in a baseball cap as he'd handed over his prized possession but not at the image of Levi. What was she doing heading off into the bush with a man she barely knew and didn't even trust?

Then again, there wasn't a lot she could do about it, except be constantly alert for any suspicious behaviour on his part.

Sophie jammed on her own Akubra, and thanked the last fading stars of the night she'd worn sturdy walking shoes, something she needed most places in the Kimberley.

During the night they'd all managed to sleep in snatches after the emotional trauma of the day, and even Odette, apart from the indigestion and backache she normally suffered from, didn't seem any worse for the experiences of the day before.

'Your baby must be one tough little munchkin, Odette,' Sophie said, as she finished her weak tea from the one shared tea bag discovered at the bottom of her bag and boiled over the campfire.

'Tougher than his mother,' Odette said with a wobble in her voice. The young mum's eyes were heavily shadowed and her fingers stroked her belly, as if to reassure herself and her baby that everything would be fine.

Sophie tamped down her own misgivings. Odette and her baby were the greatest worry. 'I think you're holding up amazingly well.' She tipped out the dregs and rinsed the one cup before she slid her bag over her shoulder. 'We'll be as quick as we can. Your baby needs you to be calm. We've done the hard part and survived the landing. You'll have something to tell the grandchildren about in thirty years.'

'If I have grandchildren.'

Sophie frowned. 'You've water and some food and a safe place.' She paused. 'No matter what happens, don't leave this spot,' Sophie reminded her. 'Sighting of the crash site is still the most probable way for rescue, and lost in the bush is the easiest way to die.'

Odette scrubbed her eyes again and the mascara from yesterday was giving her a sad-and-sorry panda look. 'I'm not going anywhere but I wish I'd never left home.'

Sophie felt the loss of the woman who'd touched up her lipstick at the clinic only a few short days ago. 'I know. It's natural to worry about your baby. You're the one with most to fear. But hey, I'd like to think I'd do as well as you are.'

Odette sniffed. 'You wouldn't cry like I do.'

Sophie hugged her and whispered, 'Didn't you see me yesterday after setting William's shoulder? I was a mess.'

Odette scrubbed her eyes with the back of her hand and peered at Sophie, who nodded. 'Really? I didn't see that.'

'Good,' Sophie said and looked around to make sure none of the men had heard. 'But I felt better afterwards.'

'I'll never be as strong as you but thanks for telling me. It helps to know I'm not the only one who can't help it sometimes.'

'I know. And I'm not that strong. Just on the outside.' Sophie glanced at her brother, who was probably giving Levi some pointers as well. 'Look,' she said. 'This isn't going to happen, but if you do go into labour, stay cuddled up to William. He'll look after you. Rest and remember you're designed to do it. Be calm and let it happen. Babies only need to be next to their mother. And remember, first babies take a long time and we'll be back. Don't give up on us.'

Odette shook her head and her eyes filled again with tears. 'You shouldn't go. Levi shouldn't leave me.' She clutched at Sophie's arm. 'Don't leave!'

Sophie drew the younger woman into her arms and hugged her. 'You'll be fine. We'll be back as quick as we can, but we need to walk out before it gets too hot.'

Odette started to cry and Sophie chewed her lip and glanced at Levi. She'd made everything worse.

Levi crossed to his sister and drew her into the circle of his arms. 'Shh, honey. One day away. That's all it'll take. You and William have a day on the land, relax and enjoy the scenery.'

Odette hiccoughed, 'Relax?' Her lip quivered as Levi handed her over to William to comfort. 'Please be careful,' Odette said to her brother.

He nodded. 'We'll be back for you in another chopper.'

'He'll fly back for you,' Sophie said drily. 'I'll be cheering from home.'

Odette's lips tugged in an almost smile. 'Chicken.'

'We won't be long.' Levi sighed. Such a dilemma. He hated to leave Odette, and the thought of her going into labour out here without him made him break into a cold sweat. Please God, don't let that happen. He'd spent his life trying to keep her safe and he'd failed dismally.

But he couldn't send Sophie off on her own, even though he suspected she'd be tougher in the outback than him.

He did have faith in William though—not quite sure how that happened—and they'd be as quick as they could, but there was no use waiting for a rescue that might never happen before they tried to walk out.

They left without looking back and he felt like a deserter as he followed Sophie down a natural trail. Initially he tried to choose the direction but his feet seemed to find the ground more uneven than Sophie did, and eventually he fell in behind her because it was easier going. It felt strange to let another person lead, let alone a woman.

The rocks shifted under his feet as his ankles threatened to twist on the uneven path. It made sense if the whole place was the result of erosion but it made walking fraught for injury.

When he thought about it they'd taken a lot for granted to head off into the hills. He caught up with Sophie and walked beside her. 'I've just had a nasty thought. Actually, we're relying on William's memory of a nomad's camp, from a muster that happened over a year ago?'

She glanced across at him. 'That's what we all decided on.'

He pushed aside a branch that reached across their path. 'What if the camp moved on, which I imagine is likely.'

She raised her eyebrows. 'We can hope the camp moved closer, then, and not further away.'

That was simple, he thought wryly. 'I love the way your mind works.' He bent down and picked up a walking-stick-size branch, tested it and then used it to part the grass in front.

She grinned at him and he found himself grinning back. 'Optimism is the code of the Kimberley.'

Was this woman for real? 'Spare me, Pollyanna. You just made that up.'

'Yep. But you can't change what you can't change.' She glanced around as the first rays of light warned of sunrise. 'More likely a hunter will find us than we'll find them anyway.'

He hadn't thought of that. 'Do they do that? I thought it was all in movies and fiction.'

'The medicine man knows if someone who shouldn't be there is around. I'm just hoping they find us sooner rather than later.'

The growing light allowed them to see the ground in front of them more clearly as the sun crept closer to rising. He'd be interested to see the pace she'd keep up when she could see properly. 'Can we do this? Walk out safely?'

She stopped and looked at him. 'We can be sensible, yes, and cut down the risks, but it's a big land under a bigger sun.' She glanced at the imminent sunrise. 'We should move faster while we can.'

The morning blurred into a fast-paced bushwalk.

Sophie pointed out another Gubinge tree and he began to see others now that he recognised them.

She showed him the low-growing, wide-leafed bush tomatoes, which looked more like brown raisins. 'But you have to eat the ripe ones. The green ones are toxic like green potatoes.'

She picked a few and offered him one. When he didn't look inspired she ate one herself and grimaced. 'They're talking about growing these commercially for a savoury spice. They're pretty pungent but you never know when you'll need them.'

He was over bush tucker. It was pretty hard to be the protective male when she held all the cards. A very novel experience for a man who'd always been the one people came to for help. 'Have you ever been to Sydney?' he said.

She didn't even look at him. 'No.'

'Maybe one day I'll show you my favourite restaurant. The chef is one of the top three in Australia.' He'd actually quite like that.

She looked at him as if he'd offered a space shuttle to the moon. 'You think?'

Apparently it wasn't on her wish list. She had to be good for his conceited soul. He laughed and followed her along another ridge that boarded a treeless plain he hoped they didn't have to cross, but she was heading in that direction. Assuming she knew where she was going.

Almost as if she heard his thoughts she paused. 'If

we keep the sun on our right shoulder we should be heading north. There's a dry creek bed through the middle of the plain and maybe even a few of the pools will have water in them. We'll conserve what we have and try to make it to the next gorge, and I'm expecting more water by midday. Then we'll rest.'

Unobtrusively he pulled his compass from his pocket and checked what she said. She was right! What did he expect? It was pretty different taking orders from a woman and actually not minding it.

Though he hadn't minded his first-grade teacher either. Miss Tee was a honey and the first woman he'd ever fallen in love with. Probably because she liked to take them outside for games when they got bored with English, but he did remember her long, long legs, like Sophie's. Though he conceded Sophie's legs were even better.

She walked with a loose-limbed gait, sure-footedly in her lace-up leather boots and her knee-length shorts that it seemed women wore here. And despite her determination to appear always in command, she couldn't hide her femininity. Her bottom still jiggled.

He realised how few women he'd seen since he'd been here, and they'd all been wearing those knee-length shorts. Maybe that was why she looked so good. Lack of competition. But he didn't think so. He had a feeling she'd look good on a rue in Paris. He caught her glancing at him and it made him smile more.

'What are you smiling at?'

He straightened his face. 'I've only seen four women since I arrived a week ago. And one of them is my sister.'

She flicked her brows up and down. 'Bet that's different to your usual day.' Was that sarcasm?

She had no idea what his life was like. The hours he worked. The impact of having to tell a patient he couldn't save their sight or the sight of their child—the main reason he'd been unable to get here sooner as he'd tried to clear a backlog of people who needed him desperately. How he'd started to think he'd never be able to make a dent in the need out there. 'Yeah, well, it's hard running a playboy mansion.'

She stopped and faced him. 'You run a playboy mansion?'

That actually hurt. Did she really think him that shallow? Nothing like his surgery full of people with visual nightmares. 'It was a joke.'

She brushed his comment away. 'Good. Don't worry. We get women here. When the tourist season properly starts the Gibb River Road really moves. Campers and off-road vehicles everywhere and the resorts fill up. You'll see plenty of ladies then, if you're still here.' She started walking again and he nearly missed her final comment. 'Which you shouldn't be for someone just passing through.'

She'd brought it up again. Wait till she found out about the other, but he didn't have the energy to go into why he didn't want to talk about work. 'Are you ever going to forgive me for a throwaway comment?'

She looked at him innocently. 'Sure. Nothing to forgive. I just don't trust you.'

Be warned, he told himself. To her, he said, 'Nice.'

She ignored his comment and went back to their original conversation. 'The tourist season is only for a few months from April until the humidity comes back again in October-November. Most people leave then because a person sweats like a horse as soon as they step outside.'

He thought about what she said, wondered about the implications on the health resources from the influx of older travellers for such small amounts of health personnel, but if he commented he might end up embroiled in more lies. Better to leave well enough alone, which was a shame, because he'd begun to value her opinion on a lot of things.

They walked on for an hour without talking and surprisingly it was quite companionable. He couldn't remember the last time he'd been with a woman without feeling he had to make the running or listen to a one-way conversation.

He looked to the scenery ahead and there was more of the same to come. 'So tell me about the camp we're heading to.'

She jolted out of her reverie. 'The family tribe we're looking for is semi-nomadic most of the year. They've returned to the old ways and move with the food, so that means berries available, fattest kangaroos, and they rely on guessing the weather.'

He glanced at the bare plains. 'Do they come into town much?'

'The young men muster when needed and that's how Smiley knows about them. I haven't actually met this family but they'd have met other nurses from other towns. I'd like to see if they want the kids immunised and all's well, so it's a bonus.'

He bit back another laugh. A bonus helicopter crash. So pleased he could accommodate her. He'd never understand her.

They walked until the sun was directly overhead and with relief they entered the foothills of the next range and what little shade that offered.

He was determined he wasn't going to ask for a rest, but he'd used most of his water, except for a little he kept in case she needed it. Not that he imagined she'd ask. But enough unusual things had happened to them over the past twenty-four hours; he wasn't guaranteeing they wouldn't have more excitement.

'There looks to be a subtropical pocket ahead, that's promising,' she said, and he could hear the note of weariness in her voice. Strangely, his own tiredness seemed to melt away and he quickened his step. 'Let me lead for a while—I can see where you mean—and you might catch a little shade from my back.'

'I'm fine.'

'I know. You're amazing. Let me do this bit until we stop. Give me your pack.' When she hesitated, he added, 'For goodness sake, let me feel a little useful.'

'Fine.' She stopped and he overtook her, glancing at her face as he passed. Her cheeks were pink with the heat, and she didn't meet his eyes, but she looked tired, then he was past and she fell into step behind him.

Within half an hour they'd moved from the grass of the plains to the spiral Pandanas of the semi-rainforest, and not much further on they found larger boulders and finally a small pool of algoid water.

The creek bed sloped up the gully and Sophie pointed to the narrowing gorge higher up. 'If we climb a little we'll find cleaner water, and it's probably worth the effort. We'll stay here for a couple of hours until the sun is well behind our backs.'

They both needed to rest, which would be hard with the idea of Odette still back at the wreck site, but Sophie was as aware of that as he.

'No problem,' Levi said. 'You said you'd find water. This place is amazing.' He looked around at the narrow strip of tropical foliage which seemed so out of place in the arid areas they'd just trekked through. There was a definite line where wet met dry and the rest of the gorge stretched away from them back to the plain of red dirt and spinifex.

He heaved himself up and around a few larger boulders and the subtle sound of running water gurgled more loudly.

'The flow must have disappeared into an underground creek because there's no flow further down,' she said.

He looked back and all he could see, water wise, was the green pool. She was a cluey little thing.

One last steep-sided boulder, room-size, stood between them and a ring of promising palm trees, but it was too high to step up onto. He wedged himself between the gorge wall and the boulder and crab walked up the gap, and he was quietly pleased he'd mastered the indoor rock climbing he enjoyed in his youth. Crumbly rock grated against his arm as he heaved himself up and it felt good to do something physical apart from walking. When he craned his neck back the sky was decorated with a palm tree on an impossible angle that arched for the sun.

Then he was up. Not easy but worth it. 'This is great,' he called down to her. The rocky pool lay fringed with ferns. Set deep in the gully under the fuzzy roots of an outstretched palm was a big bath-size rock pool catching the water from above.

'The water's clean and deep.'

When he turned to offer his hand, he expected her to shimmy up with his support, but she hesitated and turned her head to search for an alternative route, which was crazy when he could see her shoulders droop with weariness. Stubborn little thing.

He felt another spurt of impatience with her reluctance to touch him. His hand fell as he considered her refusal. There was a limit to independence. He'd thought they'd got over that in the walk. Some of his pleasure in the spot dissipated but he tried to keep his voice reasonable.

'I don't bite.' He held his hand out again. 'There's a nice pool up here. Why skin your knees when I can help you up?'

She brushed the hair from her face and looked at him, as if measuring the danger, and the skidding of her eyes confirmed it was the idea of contact that had her worried. He didn't get it.

'You're right,' she said. Finally she took his hand, and he was surprised at how much that meant that she'd decided to trust him. It was a beginning but he wasn't sure of what.

He lifted her easily, which helped his ego no end, and he acknowledged to himself he was a sad case, until she was balanced on the rock beside him and could see the pool and the tiny waterfall at one end.

'Nice.' A tired smile. 'Thanks,' and she moved from him to the other side of the pool, well away from his zone.

They both looked at the pool, he from his side and she from hers. Tiny fish flickered at the edge of the water and the gurgle of the water over rocks from the waterfall dominated the sounds of the bush.

He crouched down and rinsed his water bottle before he drank deeply, then refilled the one in his bag as well. She did the same and he looked across the small expanse of water at her bent head. He didn't get why she was so quiet. 'Is there something you're worried about or not telling me?'

She jumped. He saw it. 'What?' Her voice faltered

and then strengthened. 'You mean apart from falling out of the sky? Or having to trek in the sun through a desert to get help?' She raised her eyebrows. 'No. Why should I be worried?'

She had a point but the answer was too glib. He guessed her issues weren't for sharing, then. 'Fine.' He should leave her be, stop trying to get her attention. The woman could make him edgy and awkward like a pimply teenager and he didn't like the sensation. He undid his laces and slipped off his boots and socks. Then he pulled his shirt off. When he reached for his shorts she squeaked and he looked across.

Her eyes had widened. 'What are you doing?'

He stopped and looked around for a reason he shouldn't. 'Bathing. I'm hot and bothered and it looks good.' He raised his eyebrows. 'Is there a problem?'

'Only if you take much more off.' She looked away. 'I'm not used to men stripping in front of me.'

No one had ever complained about his body before. He slid his shorts down and stepped out of them. His boxers were black and perfectly discreet. 'I'll keep that in mind,' he said as he balanced precariously on the uneven stones at the edge of the pool. He realised he had his belly sucked in and almost blew it by laughing out loud. She wouldn't be looking anyway.

He'd turned into a peacock but reality was bringing him down. 'These rocks are nasty on bare feet.' In fact, they hurt like hell as he tried to ease into the water without damage to his toes. The rocks shifted and poked him, as if they were intent on unbalancing him.

He'd have to describe the smile she gave him as evil. 'Yes, aren't they?' She sat without making any move to undress.

She had to be as hot as he was. 'You coming in?'

'I'll see if anything bites you first.' Her voice was deadpan and he had no idea if she was serious or not.

Nice. 'What happened to the lady who said I did a good job of landing the chopper?'

Sophie didn't know. All of a sudden she was fighting to keep distance from him and it was getting harder and harder. She wasn't sure when it happened. Just little moments from after the crash when he'd given her that extra bit of support. An embrace, held her shirt.

Or this morning when she knew he'd be as hot as she was, and never complained once so that she had to keep reminding herself that he was from the city and wasn't used to their headlong scramble over the plains and gorges. He probably worked out on some treadmill in a swanky gym for hours like Brad had.

But she thought the big moment had been when he'd suggested she walk behind him to shade her from the sun and offered to carry her bag. The idea was sweet, and thoughtful, useless because the sun had been overhead, but still… Then that was followed by the constant view of sinewy ripples of muscle in his shoulders through his shirt and strong, determined thighs in his jeans as he walked ahead of her. Not fair.

How was a girl supposed to keep her head when he looked so darn strong and confident? She was tired and starting to doubt that she would be able to find the tribe and shouldn't have agreed to leave Odette in case she birthed with just Smiley there.

And just now, when he'd reached down with those big, capable hands, when he was supposed to be city soft and reliant on her, she knew if she let him she'd just sail to the top of the rock with no effort. That was when she'd got scared. When she'd started to realise he was occupying too much of her mind space.

In fact, nearly all of her mind, as she blanked out the horror of the past twenty-four hours and the fear that she'd made some dangerously bad decisions.

That sort of thing would make you think of mortality, with the good things in life she'd like to taste before the end.

But this wasn't the end. This was just a scary interlude and they would get help, and Odette would be fine. Levi and his sister would fly back to Sydney in a few days and everyone in the Kimberleys would forget them. Even Sophie Sullivan. And they would forget her.

Levi's voice broke into her thoughts. 'I said, nothing bit me, are you coming in?'

She wouldn't mind but it was a very small pool. 'It looks cold.'

CHAPTER SEVEN

LEVI floated on his back which gave her too good a view of his chest and shoulders. She swallowed. She'd known it. Levi without his shirt was a bad thing. 'Deliciously cool and I feel one hundred percent better than I did before I got in,' he said lazily.

His hair was plastered to his head and droplets ran down his strong chin and dripped onto his chest, and she couldn't help comparing him to Brad. Poor Brad.

Levi had corded bulk, not just smooth skin, and the ripples and dips of his six-pack made even Smiley look like a kid. Her stomach knotted and she looked away. She'd never seen such a discreetly muscular man in her life and no matter how much she tried to lie to herself she couldn't help but find him powerfully attractive.

If she got in she could float with her face away from him, whereas it would look silly for her to turn her back now, and he'd already seen her bra.

'Turn around, then.' She waited until his water-speckled back teased her again and then hurriedly stripped off her shoes and socks and trousers, and draped her shirt close to the edge where she could get it as soon as she left the water.

She eased herself down on her bottom. She'd been bruised before by the piled rocks getting into pools, and local knowledge suggested sliding in from a low height.

The bottom of the pool would only be waist height if she were to stand but deep enough to hide under, and oh so cool and wonderful after the distance they'd walked in the heat this morning.

The water eddied up her legs and thighs with delicious coolness. Her breath sucked in as the water passed her stomach and breasts, and then came the final shiver as she submerged her shoulders until only her nose and eyes were showing. Not much for him to look at.

She surfaced her mouth again, enough to say, 'I'm in,' and then sank back to nose level.

'You sure you can breathe?' His eyes laughed at her and his mouth curved in that killer smile she'd known would be lethal. Now he had to pull that one out of his arsenal. Darn him.

'What happens if I make a wave?' He crossed his hands and threatened to ripple the water and sink her.

She tried to imagine him as a scrubby toddler, as Odette's teasing brother, as anything but the hunk across from her. She pulled her mouth out of the water. 'Some boys never grow up. Once a bully, always a bully. I bet you were the head of the pack at school. One of those boys who tell everyone else what to do.'

They'd floated quite close now—she on her front using her hands along the bottom in the shallow places to drift around the pool. The brilliant idea of maintaining distance and turning her back had been forgotten as she waited, surprisingly intrigued, for him to answer.

A shadow passed his face. 'Being at the top of the pile is much more comfortable than being on the bottom. But I'm not a bully.'

She sniffed and paddled some more. 'That's what all bullies say.'

He shook his head. 'My father bullied my mother, even into another baby when she wasn't well enough to have one—Odette—until it killed her, and I swore I'd never condone it. Apparently my grandfather, a very rich man who didn't need to be grasping, was not a nice person either, so maybe he got it from there.'

A tantalising glimpse at the life of Levi the child was not something she'd expected and it touched a maternal instinct bone she didn't know she had. And didn't need. Please don't tell me more. She didn't want to know. Really she didn't.

A wild budgerigar, bright green and busy, hopped with his mate and chattered in a tree above their heads and she gazed up at it, trying to form the sentence to change the subject. 'Did he make life hard for you?' Not the words she intended.

'Not me. While I was young and vulnerable I wasn't there enough to be harmed by my father. I had an older brother who bore the brunt in holidays. Kyle was one of life's gentle men who shielded me. He made sure I knew the difference between good and bad behaviour and what was right. I'm eternally grateful to him for that.'

'You said "had"?'

He looked through her. 'He died, when I was thirteen. He had macular degeneration, went blind, then stepped out in front of a truck. My father said Kyle knew the truck was coming. I called him a liar.' He fingered the scar on his chin.

Sophie wanted to reach out and comfort him. 'What do *you* say?'

He focused on her face. 'Never. Kyle hated being blind but he loved us too much to think of leaving us alone.'

She could easily imagine how awful it would be for a young boy losing his big brother, after losing his mother.

'I took over the protector role and made sure Odette was never worried by him.' He rubbed the scar again and she wondered if that was how he got it. No wonder he worried about Odette. He'd feel he had to do for her what Kyle had done for him.

'That's a terrible tragedy for your family to go through.'

He shrugged. 'Even the strongest of us are shaped by events in our childhood.' He shook the droplets of water from his hair as if to shake off the past. 'What about you? There's just you and William?'

She sank back further in the water, loosening her neck as she realised she'd tensed her shoulders while he'd shared his past. 'Just Smiley and me. Our parents died four years ago—truck accident—so I guess we were lucky we weren't children. Smiley's easy to live with and we both have work we love.'

'Smiley. Great name.'

A vision of her brother, tall and serious, with just a twinkle in his eye to let her know he found something she'd said amusing, was the one solid thing in her life. The one person she could trust. But she couldn't quiet that voice that said there were facets in Levi that appealed to her, and not just the external ones, and maybe she could learn to trust him too.

He floated to the edge of the pool and rested his back against a flat rock while he considered her. 'So who let you down and broke your heart?'

Just when she thought she might trust him. 'What makes you think my heart's been broken?'

He shrugged. 'OK. So who let you down?'

She never talked about it. Smiley hadn't asked. Her friend, Kate, had a new baby on the way and was immersed in her new husband. Kate didn't need Sophie's baggage. She'd come back from Perth and buried the lot.

Suddenly it was easy to talk. 'Some guy I worked with.' Was he really interested in this? She glanced across at him and then away. Something in his face told her he hadn't asked her lightly. That he genuinely wanted to understand and she guessed it would help explain why she was the way she was.

The picture of Brad in her mind wasn't quite as sharp as it had been. One good thing. 'He was the head of Obstetrics, in my training hospital actually. Born in Australia but his parents were wealthy immigrants. He never talked about where their money came from. I guess he grew up with different values than I did.'

'In what way?' He asked the question quietly, not demanding. If she didn't want to answer she didn't have to, but maybe she needed to clarify what went wrong in her own mind.

'The way he treated people.' Yep, that was what she'd disliked the most. 'Like they were servants under his feet. He wanted old money joined with his new wealth. I kept telling him I had no money, but he was so impressed that my great-great-grandfather was one of the first settlers in Western Australia. Kept telling people when he introduced me. That I had a history his family didn't have. Had this funny idea that because two generations ago my great-grandfather opened up the Kimberleys it made me almost outback royalty.'

'Princess Sophie,' he teased.

'Yeah, right. Not a lot of call for a crown out here in the heat and the dust.'

He shredded a leaf while he listened. 'So what attracted you to him?'

She looked past Levi into the fronds behind him. 'The usual, I guess. Not that I'd actually fallen for anyone like him before. He was good-looking, quite powerful, and in the beginning he wanted to do the things I really enjoyed.' She shrugged. 'He courted me—the old-fashioned way—and I liked that.' She avoided his eyes. 'I'm not a person who is easy with casual sex.'

She looked up to see him slap his own hand. 'I'd never have guessed.' She'd swear he was laughing at her but it was strangely liberating to say the things she hadn't said out loud before.

She pulled a face. 'And you're a smart alec.'

He held his hands up. 'I'm sorry. Couldn't resist. So what happened?'

She couldn't believe she was talking about this. 'He changed. Oh, he started off doing the things I wanted to do. Walks, sailing, museums, but really he wanted great restaurants, opening-night shows, to be seen. To show me off on his arm. Don't get me wrong, that was nice too, but when I agreed to marry him it was as if he lost respect for me. I became his property.' And he demanded the sex I hadn't felt ready for, but she didn't say that. 'I had to wear the clothes he bought me. Sign the prenuptial agreement. He'd check my jewellery and shoes and handbag and make sure I had it all co-ordinated. Had to attend the chosen beauty salon once a week, and he began to talk about me giving up my job.'

Levi whistled. 'That's a few rules.'

'Tell me about it.'

Then Levi asked, 'Did you ever love him?' She

really didn't know. She'd thought she had, would have sworn it when they became engaged, but she could see now the unease that had grown enormous had always been there from the beginning.

'I must have because I put up with my reservations by thinking he knew better. Then he began to phone me any time day or night on my mobile. Keeping track. Started this campaign of speak when spoken to.'

'That must have been hard.' Levi tried to keep the smile hidden but he could feel his lips twitch.

She frowned and then reluctantly smiled. He guessed she hadn't succeeded. 'My word it was.'

Not a nice man for Sophie. No wonder she jumped half the time. Levi knew those kinds of men. Image was all-important. And the women had to be aware of the rules. Rules that didn't apply to the men.

He asked the hard one. 'And was he faithful?'

'I thought so.' She looked away. 'I was a fool.'

Levi saw the flash of hurt. The fact that she went on said a lot for her strength and honesty and he had a sudden desire to meet and deal with the jerk for her. And comfort Sophie.

'He'd been sleeping with his secretary the whole time. So everyone knew. He'd told more lies than rocks in this pool.' She glanced at the pebble-lined bath they lay in. 'Apparently it'd been going on for years but he'd never offered to marry her.' Sophie shook her head. 'What offended me the most was his girlfriend wasn't good enough to marry—only to sleep with. Creep.'

Maybe Sophie had given him what he deserved anyway. He wouldn't put it past her. 'What did you do?'

'I sold his ring and gave the money to the homeless. I told him and then I came back home. To Smiley. Got on with my life in a place where people say what they mean and don't cheat. And with a chip on my shoulder about wealthy doctors who lie.'

Levi looked away and winced. Well, he was screwed.

She should shut up. What on earth had she told him all that for and made herself vulnerable again? It had been a dismal time. Best to change the subject.

'Home was good. My brother never said a thing. Except "shortest engagement in history." He's so dead-pan most of the time, you never know what's going on in his head, though apparently your sister can read him. I've never seen him as animated as the other night at Xanadu.'

Levi shrugged but there was a tiny frown between his eyes. 'Odette likes him a lot.'

'I don't think you could get two people more dis-similar in upbringing.' Her forehead wrinkled despite the effort not to. So Levi recognised her misgivings and maybe had a few of his own. Good. It would never work.

Levi shook his head. 'Before she met the father of her baby I'd agree with you. That's my greatest regret so far, that I didn't keep her safe from men like him. Tom was a dangerous and malicious clown and no loss to his unborn child, I'm afraid. I think your brother is restoring Odette's faith in chivalrous men.' He grinned. 'And she's pregnant. No harm can be done.'

Chivalrous. Such an old-fashioned word but, in this context, perfect. The description of Smiley. 'Are you chivalrous?' It popped out like froth from the waterfall and subtly the mood in the pool changed.

'Sometimes. Before I became tired and jaded.'

She let his words flow over her to think about later. Suddenly she was thinking about the way his mouth moved and that curve to his lips that she was finally seeing more of. He'd been expressionless most of the time since that first day.

Originally she'd thought him moody but apparently he'd been worry worn. Well, he was pretty focused right now. She could feel the brush of his perusal as he tilted his head and smiled with that devilish curve to his dangerous mouth.

Time to break back to the previous mood, she thought with a little spurt of panic. 'So what made you tired and jaded?'

The smile straightened and disappeared. 'Someone died two years ago. In a way that affected how I thought about my achievements. I've been running on the treadmill since. But I won't bore you with it.'

Boring me might be safer, she thought but she didn't say it. Couldn't make the effort to turn the tide of awareness she'd begun to drift in.

He floated across the pool and closed in on her. His

eyes seemed darker and his lips parted as if he might whisper something—or do something else...

'I must admit I feel more alive than I have in a long time,' he said, and she felt the pricks of gooseflesh along her shoulders and arms.

She tried to move away but her body felt so heavy in the water she barely moved. Sound had receded and even the water temperature faded. 'Might be something to do with the fact we nearly died yesterday.' Now her voice sounded breathy and unsure.

'No doubt.' He sank under the water until not just his strong, brown shoulders were under but his chin as well. Just his angular face showed through, shadowed by the overhanging palms that darkened the planes of his cheeks. 'It's good to be alive.' He pursed his lips and blew a leaf across the water towards her. The leaf spun and twisted and bumped against her chin.

It was just a leaf. She could feel her heart thundering under the water. His gaze locked with hers, and it was as if he blew the air over her skin, but that was ridiculous. She was under the water, for goodness sake.

Yet here she was, with tiny flutters of heated awareness in a cold pond of sudden desire. It shouldn't have been erotic. But it was. A stranger, in a strange place, and strange feelings she hadn't experienced before. Enough to kick in her belly and make her aware of the fullness in her breasts and the beat of her heart.

Then his breath rippled across the water to tickle her face. She moistened her lips to say something inane, but before she could form the words he'd drifted closer until their noses touched with a little bump, like two leaves in a deserted pond, and she shivered.

All the time he stared into her eyes, and she could do little but breathe in and out and stare back and wonder at the dozen different blue rings inside his eyes and those dark, dark lashes drawing her closer.

She knew he was going to kiss her. Should be backing away when, in fact, she was drawn towards him by the primitive magnetism she had no control over.

When his mouth finally touched hers it was incredibly slow and gentle, an open-mouthed brush of his lips that impacted like an earth tremor against hers, and her lids drooped as she breathed in. His mouth slid to her cheek and down her neck, darting electrical tremors along her arms and legs that sent waves of mingled breath and kicks of desire back up into her chest. The sensations expanded in seismic rings of awareness and lust, and suddenly it was closer she needed to be, not further away.

Then he returned, took her mouth and enslaved her with a long draught from a well she hadn't known she had that meshed their souls in this primitive place, a day after they'd nearly died. Somehow, with that potent kiss, he touched the part of her that no one, not even Brad, had ever touched...and she was his. That simple and that complicated.

Immersed in sensation, she sighed as his hands slid from her shoulders down past her waist until he cupped both hips and pulled her toward him. Somehow, her fingers became entangled in his thick hair and luxuriated in the springiness as her breasts were squashed against his chest.

Time passed, moment by glorious moment, and she slipped deeper and deeper under his spell until she realised she was clutching at him as he tried to pull back.

She opened her eyes, focused and, horrified, she jolted herself away and would have moved further if he hadn't put his hand out and stilled her.

'It's OK. It's just a kiss. You're so beautiful,' he said, his voice heavy and deep, and she shuddered another breath in as he lifted a strand of hair off her forehead before he pulled back and floated away. And left her bereft.

The blood pounded in her ears and she watched him, like a rabbit in headlights, mesmerized, as he increased the distance between their bodies. Gradually she began to feel the world again and with it the sounds of the birds overhead and the wind in the leaves and the thunder of her heart.

Levi forced himself away. God, she was beautiful. And luscious and so, so ripe for the taking. And he wanted her. There was no doubt about that, but what the hell was he doing? There was no future in this, just heartbreak for Sophie, and maybe even for him.

It was lucky this pool was cold, which would help, but even then he'd have to stay submerged till he had himself under control. He nearly lost himself—both of them. It would only have taken another minute to pass the point of no return, and she was too innocent and trusting to realise.

He guessed he wasn't chivalrous.

He fisted his hands under the water and forced himself to calm. What had he been thinking? Fool. Of course, he hadn't been thinking—he'd been feeling, in-dulging in a daydream, or more like an erotic fantasy to play nymphs and satyrs in an oasis. A great way to say thank-you to the woman trying to save them all. But she'd looked so kissable with her satin skin and fine-boned shoulders that it made him ache like he hadn't ached for years. If he were honest, he'd wanted to kiss her since the night she'd come to Xanadu. Do more than kiss, and he'd very nearly had his way. She would have hated him. He would have hated himself.

The silence between them was broken only by the noisy budgerigar and his mate. Levi floated with his back to her while she climbed out, carefully, so as not to hurt her feet.

Sophie's hands shook, were stupidly clumsy as she wiped herself over with her shorts, and her lower limbs still wobbled as she redressed damply. Still in a daze from one kiss? A mouth-tingling caress like nothing she'd ever experienced before.

Sleazebag Brad had been practised, smooth and—now she could see—one dimensional, not like Levi, a city marauder of devastating understatement and finesse.

She shivered, not with cold, but with new knowledge of greater danger. Where was the line between attraction and wanting to be lost in a man's arms and the terrible danger of falling in love? She knew how much pain that could cause.

Her damp shirt stuck to her bra and outlined her nipples and she pulled the material out from her body to air it. It would dry all too quickly when they crossed the next plain but it embarrassed her horribly at this moment. She settled herself facing the gorge they'd climbed and breathed slowly and carefully to regain her composure. She could do that.

Still she couldn't look to the pool at Levi. Her lips thrummed as if she'd just eaten a Kakadu plum. When, in fact, she'd tasted something much better.

The water splashed behind her and a muffled curse forced a reluctant smile. He'd stubbed his toe. Good. Take his mind off kissing her.

She dug in her bag and pulled out the chocolate bar. It bent in her hand, soft and squishy, and she looked at it with a sigh. Hot chocolate was good in winter, and even like this when you hadn't had anything to eat since a tart piece of fruit. Something to take her mind off other parts of her body. The paper ripped in her teeth and the first sweet taste oozed onto her tongue.

She sucked the wrapper as she considered their options. Anything not to think of the pool and what passed between them. They'd cross the plain in the afternoon sun and hopefully find the camp before dark. That was the scary part. If they didn't...

CHAPTER EIGHT

BY TWO they were on their way again and nothing was said of the kiss in the pool. The heat bit into Levi's shoulders through his shirt and the grass crunched drily under their feet. The plain stretched ahead of them in a seemingly endless roll with stunted trees and anthills their only shade.

Levi could feel the difference—the awareness between them had increased, the air vibrated and not just with heat from the sun. He'd caused this. Created her distress. He could regret implementing the kiss but not the kiss itself because there was something about that moment that said it had to be. But his stupid lack of control had caused her discomfort. He needed to find some way to lighten the strain between them. 'So what's with the big anthills?'

She jumped when he spoke. He wished she wouldn't do that. Not for the first time wondered whoever that bloke was he'd like to have a go at him.

'Termite mounds. Not anthills.'

He looked again. Termite mounds, then. Everywhere, from small bumps in the dirt to huge towers taller than a man. Even on the cliff faces when he looked.

More interesting than he expected. 'So tell me about termites.'

She stopped and put her hands on her hips. 'What makes you think I know?'

She had a cute pose. 'You know everything.'

'You are so full of—'

'Ah-ah.' He shook his finger at her and cut her off. 'So you don't know?'

She sighed. 'Termites are blind.' She may pretend to be resigned but he saw the lessening of tension in her and it made him feel good about himself. Strange.

She went on and he smiled at the way she loved to explain things. It was one of those little things he'd grown to recognise and like about her. The passion for her world. He didn't see a lot of passion where he'd come from. Just day-in, day-out twelve-hour days. Certainly he hadn't exhibited any for a while, probably not for a couple of years. Well, not that kind anyway.

'Termites are opaque and the workers can live for thirty years.' She gave him a tentative smile. 'The queen can live eighty years.'

Nice smile. 'That'd be right. Poor man doing all the work.' He gestured to the adult-size tower of dirt. 'So what are these made of?'

She rolled her eyes at him. 'Mounds are made with saliva, spinifex, mud and termite poo, and they grow at a rate of about one foot every ten years.' She pointed to a mound that was broken. 'You can tell when they're abandoned because an active mound that's broken is repaired very quickly.'

He whistled and patted a six-foot mound they were passing. 'There're a lot of years here.'

She paused and looked around with that passion shining from her eyes. 'The story of the Kimberleys—lots of years. This whole area is the product of erosion of a giant mountain range, the Leopold, millions of years ago. That's why the ground's so rocky.'

And why not much grew around here, he guessed. 'So no bushrangers right out here in the past?'

'Not so much bushrangers, not enough people to rob, but there's a story about an escapee who killed a policeman and hid the body inside a termite mound.'

The woman was a mine of scary information. 'Don't tell me. The termites repaired the mound and he was never found.'

'You got it.'

She made him smile. Suddenly, most of the time. Even through this disaster. 'So I'd better not annoy you.'

She showed her teeth. 'Or you'll never be found.'

Sophie had sealed what had happened between them at the pool like the termites sealed their mounds, but she still felt embarrassed that she'd let him kiss her. She didn't have the headspace for the questions that had arisen from that kiss. She was focused now on getting home. Desperately.

She was doubly glad of his environmental interest because she could feel the fear build as the day lengthened. She'd been fairly confident this morning, and still sure they would find the camp at lunch, but this afternoon her water bottle emptied and conversation between them dried up like the sweat on their bodies, and she began to worry about their options.

She must have sighed because he looked across at her and touched her shoulder. 'What's wrong?'

She stopped and unconsciously her hand came over the top of his for comfort. 'It's taking longer than I'd hoped.'

He turned her into his chest and moved so she was out of the sun behind his body—a different type of embrace than the last one she didn't want to think about—and she rested her forehead on him for a moment. His voice rumbled in his chest. 'We'll find them, if not today, then tomorrow. If we don't, we know we can make it back to the others.'

Could they? She thought about how far they'd walked. Yes, they could. She could almost feel the strength transferring from him to her. His confidence boosted hers, probably unjustifiably, not that she wanted him to tell her otherwise. She had enough doubts for both of them.

Her stomach growled. 'I don't know about you but I'm getting hungry,' she mumbled into his shirt.

'Where's a drive-through Gubinge tree when you want one?' He kicked the ground. 'There's always the grubs. Ten fat ones a day, did you say?'

She had to laugh. Or she'd cry. But she did feel better. Then he put her away from him and dug in his pocket. He held up his liquid chocolate bar. 'I was saving this one for you.'

She shook her head vehemently. 'I'm not eating your chocolate.'

'Sure you are.' He pointed to the hills up ahead. 'We'll stop there and fight about it.' Then he patted her hair and took her pack from her back and captured her fingers. 'Let's go.' He pulled her fingers gently, and suddenly the strength came back along with her focus, and she walked beside him with their hands swinging together over the red earth.

She didn't know when it happened but suddenly she did trust him. Was happy to allow him to shoulder some of the burden, something so out of character for her she didn't understand how he'd achieved it. Especially after the kiss. Or was it because of the kiss?

They were close to the last foothills when the Aboriginal elder appeared. His wizened skin crinkled in mahogany folds and his grey hair hung long and straggled. Levi saw him standing beside a termite hill before Sophie did.

He carried a spear for hunting and little else.

Levi stopped suddenly when he saw him but Sophie kept going. 'He wants us to follow him.'

Levi glanced across at her. 'Guess you were right again.'

Sophie sighed with relief. Not before time. They were running out of afternoon. She'd done one thing right, then. 'This was a good one to win.'

The elder took them to a side gully and presented them with another fresh pool to drink and cool themselves. He didn't speak and she watched Levi, with hidden amusement, as he attempted to sign their story but the old man just stared at him.

'I doubt he's learnt English for the little use he'd have for it.' She handed him a stick. 'Maybe if you drew a picture in the sand?'

Levi's sand helicopter left a lot to be desired but a broad grin from the elder seemed as though he'd figured where they'd come from. Levi drew four people and then pointed to himself and Sophie, indicating the other two were still at the helicopter.

The old man nodded, seriously, and pointed to the sun and then an arc in the sky to almost sunset, and gestured they follow him, and that they'd be able to get back to the others after that.

Sophie didn't know if it was her imagination, or just the relief, but the walking was less strenuous, more shaded, and yet seemed as though they covered more ground.

An hour before sunset they came to the camp, a collection of half a dozen lean-tos, with several brown-eyed, brown-skinned toddlers scuffling in the dust.

It was unusually quiet and a quorum of women seemed congregated around a lean-to at the end of the camp. The hair on Sophie's arms stood up. Something was wrong. She glanced at Levi, who raised his brows and shrugged. He could sense it too.

The oldest lady pointed to her. Sophie approached them diffidently, used to not catching the elder's eyes. The lady, probably the grandmother, pointed her finger at Sophie. 'You that nurse, sheila, eh?' She gestured into the lean-to with her head.

Weariness swamped her and Sophie forced her head to lift as she glanced back at Levi. It seemed this day had more in store for her. Lord knew what she'd discover and it seemed she would soon find out.

He took a step to follow her. 'Do you want me to come with you?' But the old lady gestured him away.

Sophie sighed. 'Nice thought but it's not going to happen. I'd say it's secret women's business.' Sophie bent and followed the woman inside, and her heart bumped at the thought of the unknown and what might be expected of her.

The air inside the lean-to was stifling; the place seemed full of aunties and the grandmother. The young girl who lay on the dry grass bed looked more like a frightened rabbit than a woman about to give birth.

'Oh, Lord,' Sophie muttered. The sight of one tiny baby's foot resting between the mother's legs was enough to make Sophie feel like a frightened rabbit too. Footling breech, so the baby's legs would come out long before the head. If it all went well.

'As it should,' she said out loud, to bolster her own conviction.

Of course a Caesarean section would be a nice option to have in the wings in case of complications, Sophie wished fruitlessly, but that wasn't going to happen. All she could think of was the mantra from her training—hands off the breech.

Then she saw the little foot move. So the baby was alive and the day improved enormously.

Now wasn't the time to ask why the girl wasn't near a hospital if she was close to birth time. Far too late for that. Sophie knew that sometimes the fear of being away from their families made the young women hide their pregnancies so they weren't sent away. But Sophie also knew the girl would be in trouble with the elders later.

She knelt down and tried for a smile, then tapped her own chest. 'Sophie.'

The older lady pointed to the girl. 'Pearl.'

'Hello, Pearl,' Sophie said, but Pearl's frightened brown eyes skittered to the gaggle of aunties and refused to return. Sophie gestured for permission to feel the mother's abdomen and the grandmother shooed her on to the task as if to say hurry up.

Pearl's baby seemed smaller than term, which could be a good thing, or maybe it was just because it was breech and a lot of the baby was already in the pelvis. Pearl was fine boned with no extra weight, and Sophie would love to have known how long the labour had been going on.

The next contraction arrived and Pearl screwed her face up and whimpered with the pain. Her baby's little foot descended another centimetre into the world.

At this moment there wasn't much Sophie could do except be there for the end. And pray. She couldn't listen to the baby's heartbeats because she didn't have any form of stethoscope. She didn't have gloves, nor could she even wash her hands, but she couldn't leave Pearl alone either.

Levi's support was denied because culturally Pearl's birthing was women's business and men were banned. Though, if she had a problem when the baby arrived, Sophie knew darn well she'd be yelling for Levi.

Just knowing he was there gave immense reassurance. She'd expect Levi's first-aid skills and common sense would help more than anyone else's.

She guessed that even if she'd some way to contact the Royal Flying Doctor Service the plane wouldn't be here before it was all over. So much for her brief respite from responsibility. There was nothing to be done but settle herself slightly more comfortably on the dusty floor and try to ignore the trickle of perspiration that ran down between her shoulder blades. She licked her lips and tasted the dryness of her mouth. A drink would have been good.

Sophie began to pray for a rapid second stage of labour but there was only so much praying she could do. She glanced around for something else positive to focus on and her gaze rested on a brown shawl she could dry the baby with when it was born. That was a positive thought. When it was born.

The aunties all looked at her as if she should do something and she tried to block out the thoughts that didn't help.

Thoughts about drugs, and oxygen, and paediatricians who may as well be on the moon. Hopefully the baby had grown well and wasn't too premature.

If the young mum had had no antenatal care, then she was probably anaemic to start with which increased her chance of bleeding afterwards, and any blood loss would make her dangerously depleted in red blood cells.

But there wasn't a lot Sophie could do about that either. She could rub the mum's tummy to encourage clamping down of the uterus when the placenta was delivered, and she could put the baby to the breast as soon as possible to release the natural hormones that were there to do the same thing.

Women had been birthing for thousands of years in the camps, she reassured herself, well before twentieth-century medicine had decreed they were safer at the hospitals. Trouble was now the elder women had lost their skills as attendants over the past hundred years.

She needed to think of more positives. At least the

heat would make it unlikely the baby would get cold, which breech babies tended to do as their bodies waited for the heads to be born.

For some reason she thought of Levi's Pollyanna comment and it steadied her because there was nothing wrong with looking on the bright side of things.

Pearl moaned again and this time the baby's ankle came down almost to the knee and suddenly there was a second foot. 'You're doing great, Pearl.' Sophie plastered a happy face on and nodded her head at the frightened girl and her attendants. The least she could do was be supportive, instead of a harbinger of doom.

If the cervix was not fully opened, then Pearl was going to push against it anyway. If she sat up it would be easier for the baby and put even more pressure on the cervix. Sophie looked at the grandmother and gestured that they help Pearl to squat in a supported position.

Gravity would help bring the baby down and hopefully all would happen quickly before the baby's cord became too squashed by the after-coming head.

With Pearl upright her labour did seem to progress more quickly. First the baby's knees and the thighs appeared with just the change of position and then Pearl pushed until a swollen black scrotum appeared and the women broke into voluble noise and exclamations at the evidence of a new male for the family.

The elder woman gestured to Sophie to grab the baby but Sophie shook her head emphatically.

This was where "hands off the breech" was most important. Sophie knew the natural curves of the mother's pelvis shaped the baby into having his chin tucked into his chest and the arms by his side. If they pulled the baby downwards, his head would tip back into a bigger diameter and his arms might drag behind his head to create a complication that should never have happened.

'No touch,' Sophie said and waved her hands in a negative sign. 'Baby knows.'

Little skinny buttocks followed by hips, back and umbilical cord all came through next, and Sophie resisted the urge to feel the cord and check the heart rate of the baby. She'd bet it was slower than her own thumping heart was, but the less she touched, the less spasm the cord would endure.

There certainly wasn't anything else Sophie could do except prevent people pulling on the baby as he descended. She'd just ensure Pearl's baby came out with his back facing Sophie, so his head could lift from his chin-on-chest position to birth, just like a head-first baby did.

Grandmother clutched her hair and moaned, and gestured to Sophie at the paleness of the baby, and Sophie could tell she wanted to help make the baby come quicker. 'Soon,' Sophie soothed. 'All over soon.'

Sophie tried another prayer and slipped her wrist between the baby's legs so that when the chest was through and first one shoulder and then the other was born the baby was hanging all out with only the neck and head to come. Sophie's heart was thumping so loud in her ears she didn't doubt the aunties could hear, but she was strangely calm.

She allowed the weight of the baby to hang a little to ensure the head stayed deflexed until the last moment. Sophie's bent legs ached from squatting in almost under Pearl.

Now. Time to deliver the head. She placed one hand on top of the baby's shoulders and back of the neck and the other underneath on the baby's cheeks so when the head birthed it didn't spring out suddenly. The hardest part.

The baby's head had been rushed through the pelvis. To ease a baby slowly out of the constriction of the birth canal was less risky than a head being forced out quickly into sudden expansion.

'Here he comes,' Sophie muttered. She achingly raised herself from her own squat to lift the baby slowly, holding shoulders and cheeks between her hands as the baby made an arc in front of his mother's belly. His head was born with chin, mouth and nose, then eyes and finally the whole baby was out.

Pearl sagged back onto her heels and then onto her back, and Sophie wiped the still-flaccid baby over with the shawl until his little limbs contracted in reflex and he breathed. She pulled Pearl's T-shirt up and lay her son directly skin to skin across her chest.

At the first touch of his mother's skin he gasped and cried—which by this point was exactly what Sophie felt like doing herself. But there was no time for that.

Grandmother tied the twine where Sophie indicated, and the baby was totally separated from his mother by the lethal-looking knife they cut the cord with, and finally she could back away a little as the aunties crowded in.

Her hands shook and she wiped the sweat from her face with her forearm. Cord and placenta followed shortly and a gush of bright blood seeped and began to form a pool. 'Pearl—' Sophie leant in to catch the young woman's eye '—I need to rub your tummy.'

Sophie nudged the grandmother and showed her how rubbing the now-grapefruit-size uterus in Pearl's belly stopped the flow of blood until the uterus was a hard nub beneath their fingers. The grandmother nodded and brought her gnarled hand in over Sophie's. Sophie wondered if one day another woman would be as lucky if the grandmother remembered this part.

Another aunty put Pearl's baby to her mother's breast and Sophie sat back and drew a deep breath. Baby whimpered and then cried again before he latched and began to suck. They didn't need her any more and she had to get out of here before she fainted from the heat.

CHAPTER NINE

IT SEEMED hours since she'd disappeared. Levi paced himself a worn strip under the tree as he watched the opening of the humpy.

Even hand signals with the children as he attempted to take a health stock of those he could see hadn't passed the time. Eventually he'd found an elder who conversed more easily, immunisation status not something he'd normally have pursued, but Sophie wanted to know. And there was only so much washing and drinking in the creek he could do when all the time he slaked his own thirst he knew she'd be parched. At least he'd soaked a cloth and filled her bottles for when she came out.

But he should have told her earlier about his qualifications, or at least discussed where he could help. The longer she'd spent inside with the women, the deeper his guilt. An uncomfortable feeling he could have done without.

Not that he had a lot of experience with obstetrics,

except for Odette's pregnancy and one small obstetric rotation that had him back-pedalling away from something with too much emotion attached to it, but he hadn't forgotten how helpful it could be to have another medical person to discuss things with.

His own career path had opted for something he could achieve on his own, something technical he could master and something he'd decided on when his brother went blind, and he'd been very successful. Though the past two years had been hard since Darla's death, where he'd driven himself to work outrageous hours—and he'd almost burnt out, he realised now—which must be why it felt so different to smile around Sophie so often.

Then again, perhaps a near-death helicopter crash could enliven one too.

But that didn't help his guilt about Sophie. Apart from his sister, he'd been accountable to no one since his brother died. He'd disliked his father, but that was moot now. Women had been in and out of his life, but none had left him with doubts about his behaviour like this outback dynamo did.

When Sophie finally unbent herself from the humpy Levi felt the air whoosh out of his lungs as his shoulders dropped with relief. Now he could watch her draw a deep breath and gather herself. He remembered she did that a lot and it said volumes for her stamina and inner strength. Another thing he admired about her.

He'd bet the air outside seemed sweet and cooler, especially as it approached sunset. The sound of a very new baby roaring his lungs out followed her. This woman continued to amaze him.

For the briefest moment he thought he recognised something in her eyes when she looked at him that made the stress of waiting worthwhile—and brought back the guilt tenfold.

For Sophie, the sight of Levi made her want to throw herself into his arms for comfort. But she needed to wash and she needed a drink and she needed not to think about all the things that could have gone wrong that hadn't.

'Sophie?' Levi took her arm and sat her down under a tree. 'Sit.' He handed her a water bottle and she took a long drink with her eyes closed. It felt so good to be outside.

'Another amazing job?'

She opened her eyes, glanced around at the plains surrounding them and sighed. 'Footling breech. We were all lucky.' The exhaustion hit her as she sagged back against the knobbly trunk behind her.

Levi gave her a searching look. 'I'll get your other drink.' He handed her some damp cloths. 'Here's something to wash with until you're up to a walk to the creek.'

He'd torn both sleeves off his shirt and soaked them. Brilliant. Amazing. Just what she needed. When he offered them to her she could have hugged him or, for a brief, mad second, run her hands over the bulge of his upper arms that were very nicely displayed without sleeves. There was something about a man in a shirt without sleeves that called to her, not that she'd noticed that fetish before—no doubt it was especially true when that man supplied what she desperately wanted most.

It must have shown in her face because he gave her a lopsided grin. 'I've been to the shop. Maybe you'd like a Kakadu plum?'

The giggle surprised her. Probably hysteria but the release of emotion actually felt good. A little out of control, but good. He was cosseting again and she wallowed in it for a few indulgent seconds while she wiped her hands and, with a clean corner of the damp material, her face. The coolness against her forehead was worth a hundred facials Sleazebag Brad had insisted she have.

In fact, she was growing to appreciate this man more and more, though she wouldn't fall for him. But it was hard. He made her feel crazily alive and special. A safe harbour to come into. Strong arms when she needed them. But she wasn't in love. Not going there! She was very glad he was here with her though.

'There's hope for you yet.' She looked across at him but he only grimaced and her euphoria dimmed. He didn't look as happy as she felt.

Levi looked away and rubbed his neck and, to Sophie, the afternoon suddenly seemed stifling again. 'I'm glad,' he said, 'because there's something else I have to tell you.'

Lightly spoken but determined, and her stomach

sank as she wondered how much bad news a person could take in one day.

'The good news.' She was too weary for bad at this minute. 'Please.'

'From what I gather, our tracker was on his way back when he found us and the Flying Doctor is coming for your girl. We'll be able to use their radio when they land.'

Her shoulders dropped in a heartfelt sigh. Not just good. 'That's great news.' The day would work out. This whole draining adventure would end. She could get home in the not too distant future, shower and have a cup of tea, and maybe she and Levi—and the others of course, she hastened to remind herself—could share that steak she'd kill for. She didn't want to hear the bad news. She glanced around for something to divert him.

Barefoot, dark-eyed children huddled into a little giggling group to one side and darted mischievous glances across to where Sophie and Levi sat. 'Have you been making friends while I've been busy?'

He smiled at the children and pulled a silly face which sent them off into a new fit of giggles. 'So it seems.'

So he was good with kids too. She sucked her breath in and felt the warmth expand in her stomach. He really did have qualities she admired, and of course he was different to that man in her past. She shied away from the comparison, although it did Levi no disservice against Brad. It was far too early to think about the future.

She looked from him to the little brown bodies that had begun to poke and wriggle amongst themselves. These children looked lean, but full of energy. 'I wonder if the kids are up to date with their immunizations?'

'Apparently,' he said a little smugly, and she had to smile. 'I asked. And they look well.'

He'd asked? Why? Because she'd said once she wanted to know? More warm and fuzzies buzzed in her belly and she smiled up at him. 'You've been busy. Anyone I need to look at?'

He hesitated. 'There's an elder here almost blind with cataracts. He'd benefit from surgery.'

Sophie looked around the camp. Lean-tos, red dust, a couple of shady trees and the creek. 'It's hard to encourage elders to leave their home for something they've learnt to live with.'

Levi shook his head. 'He's sightless. The results would be brilliant.'

Sophie nodded. 'I know. But he has to have the money to travel to the doctor.'

'What money?' Levi looked at her. 'The operation is free in public hospitals.'

Sophie shrugged, only giving half her concentration as she began to relax. She watched the children. Sipped more water. Exhaled. The baby was fine. She'd done the right thing. And now the Flying Doctor could take over the care. She could unwind. 'He'd have to leave here, travel, live away from his family. And for these people the thought of an operation is beyond frightening.'

'It's a minor operation.' Levi was like a terrier and his intensity began to intrude on her equilibrium.

Something in the way he persisted made her look away from the children to him. She spoke slowly as the implications sparked a question, and then a creeping disquiet that maybe she'd missed something. Been blind. More blind than an elder with cataracts? And stupid? 'Do you have much experience at diagnosing cataracts?'

His eyes searched hers and she knew. Felt the red dusty world fall away from under her feet. Felt the heat in her cheeks as she flushed with embarrassment and not a little anger.

'I could have,' he said.

Her eyes narrowed as she looked into his face. The same wary expression as the first time she'd met him. The face of a liar. All the boxes slid into place in her mind—the comments, the looks between his sister and himself, his 'first aid.' She tried to keep the hurt out of her voice. 'What sort of business did you say you had?'

'I didn't.' Still he looked at her so she had to break eye contact.

'And...?' She gazed at the children across the camp.

He paused, waited until she met his eyes again. 'I'm an ophthalmologist specialising in microsurgery. I have a very successful practice in Sydney.'

'You're a doctor?' Quietly. 'You said first aid.' Her voice dropped even lower. 'You lied again.'

His voice was low too. 'I didn't lie.'

'You didn't deny.' It hurt; actually, it crushed her that she'd been fooled again. 'Liar by omission.'

'That was the bad news.'

What did he want? A pat on the head? It was bad all right. She'd started to like him. Like him a lot. Please God, not love him. She'd certainly begun to lean on him more than a little. And he was a doctor. A rich doctor. And a liar. Just like Brad. The man who'd stripped her heart, and taken a part of her that had been precious and new and untarnished, and stamped on it.

And she'd ordered Levi around because she'd been the only medical person. Did he understand how hard it had been to wear that responsibility, and now he tells her he's better qualified? Even if he was a surgeon he'd started as a generalist.

He could have put Smiley's shoulder in. The weight of unshed tears made her face feel heavy. Like a big rock tied to her cheeks, pulling her whole face down. She blinked her stupid stinging eyes and gritted her teeth. No way was she wasting water on this creep.

'I'm struggling to think of a reason you wouldn't make this all easier on me. Was this some kind of test to see how much I'd take before I broke?'

He shook his head and reached his hand out. She looked at his fingers as if they were covered in slime. He must have seen it because his hand dropped. 'Look. Sophie. I think you're amazing.' He dragged his hand through his hair. 'You didn't need my help.'

Holy cow. How dare he? She so didn't want to do this now. Or ever. She climbed wearily to her feet and with her eyes fixed past his shoulder she took off down the hill to the creek to gather herself, almost tripping in her haste to get away from him.

The water splashed cold against her fingers and she plunged her hands and forearms in to shock herself out of the stifling blanket of cotton wool she felt smothered in. She'd been so close, had almost fallen in love with exactly the type of man who could crush her—again— and in just a few short days. Didn't she learn from her mistakes?

She washed her face, washed the trickles that weren't creek water and then washed it again. Damn him.

Slowly composure returned, or at least her hands stopped shaking and her tears dried. Her head ached with a dense weariness that seemed to wrap around her bones, and she forced tired feet to carry her back to the camp. But she walked straight past him to the humpy to check the mother and baby.

By the time she emerged she had control again and an impenetrable barrier around her higher than the escarpment they'd nearly flown into. The sound of an aeroplane droned in the distance, and Sophie searched for the sight of it over the hills like she needed it to breathe.

Anything instead of looking at Levi.

The sooner that plane landed, the better. She wasn't even worried about flying out of here.

She had to think of Odette, still out in the scrub, unaware that help was coming, and the possibility of her labour. Once she was safe Sophie could release all responsibility. And she would. Posthaste.

When they made town he could worry about the disaster of the helicopter and she and Smiley could go home. With just a little luck she'd never see him again and she could forget what a fool she'd almost been.

Finally the noise of the plane dominated the sky and the shadow crossed the ground in front of them as the pilot circled to land on the area the men had cleared. Bring it on, Sophie said under her breath.

When the twin-engine aircraft landed, surprisingly smoothly on the rocky soil, the plane held three people—the doctor, Jock McDonald, a Scottish larrikin who raised his eyebrows at the sight of Levi and Sophie; the nurse, who strode purposefully towards them; and the pilot, who waved but stayed to shut the engine down.

'There'll be a story there, I'm noo doubting,' Jock said to Sophie, whom he'd met at the clinic. He waved at Levi. 'I'll talk to you in a wee moment.'

The nurse hailed Sophie and the two women accompanied Jock into the humpy, suddenly critically crowded until the doctor shooed away all except the grandmother, then checked Pearl and scolded her in such a broad accent there wasn't a hope she'd understand what he said. But he smiled and patted her head when he'd finished and again when he'd checked the tiny but vigorous baby over with obvious admiration.

'You're verra lucky. You'll both still come to the hospital so we can keep an eye on you for a day or two,' he said to Pearl and again to the grandmother, 'In case baby goes off his food. He's only a wee thing.'

Then he left the humpy and he raised his eyebrows at Sophie. 'I'd like to hear your side of it. You did well, lassie.'

Sophie didn't feel anything but tired. 'Everything went right. Hands off the breech until the head. Baby fine by a minute after birth. We weren't unlucky but we would have been up the creek if it hadn't panned out as well as it had.'

'Aye. But you weren't. So no use worryin' about the ones that go good like they're supposed to.' He pulled his hand antiseptic from his pocket and offered it to Sophie and she lathered herself. Unimaginable luxury.

Dr Jock inclined his head towards the tree. 'So who's this big fella and how're you two here?'

She shook her head. She didn't want to talk about it. 'He'll fill you in. Have you room for us?'

He looked at the plane. 'Och, no, not for two, but we can contact the Bungles and they'll fly in and get him. We'll have to take the mother and bairn or she'll have no care if either get sick.' He gave her a searching look. 'I'm thinkin' you need to come with us.' Then he crossed to where Levi was talking to the pilot under the tree with a map spread between them.

Fifteen minutes later, Sophie joined Pearl and her

baby in the RFDS plane with Dr Jock, while the nurse rode up front with the pilot.

Levi had been in contact with a helicopter service at the Bungles who were en route to pick him up. Another had flown to the crash site. More red tape would follow at a later date, but for the moment Odette and Smiley were on their way back to the hospital at Kununurra and Sophie could drop the last of her responsibilities.

An hour later she finally stepped out of the plane at the airport in Kununurra too. But it wasn't where she wanted to be. She ached to go home, back to her own space, a place to hide and lick her wounds and take stock of the new disaster she'd brought on herself, but she'd have to wait for the hospital to release her brother.

The nurse from the flight lent her flat keys and spare clothes, and Sophie spent an hour soaking red dust from her legs and her hair in a long bath that should have relaxed her but didn't.

She could hear the sound of helicopters taking off and landing at the airfield across the road and the sound grated across her ears like gravel over her skin. No doubt one of them held *him*. All the time she wished she'd never let her guard down—couldn't believe she'd done it again, fallen for the words and caresses of a smooth-talking liar. But never again.

Levi watched the entrance to the hospital as cars with lights drove up and deposited people. Watched every taxi, truck and bus that pulled up. He watched families walking and couples talking and single women who didn't matter, but nowhere did he see a ponytail in an Akubra hat that quickened his heart.

It was night now but this day never seemed to end. He'd spent an hour at the police station. The aircraft crash investigation team were coming from Perth and until then nothing could be proved, but they were on alert. He wasn't having his sister put at risk again. He'd arranged a light aircraft flight to get them all home, and told the men at Xanadu to put the lights out on the strip, as well as the men at the station township to put another set out, and he'd seen Odette and William. Neither had spotted Sophie but William had heard her on the phone.

She'd been on the ground for two hours now; he'd checked. She should be here soon.

He still didn't know what to say. She hadn't allowed him a word since he'd told her, hadn't looked at him before she left, but the hurt in her eyes had bitten harder than he'd expected. He just hoped she'd cool down and then he could explain before he had to take Odette back to Sydney.

The digital clock in the hospital foyer flashed ten past nine and a taxi pulled up. There she was. Strangely smaller than he remembered, in a pair of long trousers that didn't suit her as much as her shorts. The toss of her head when she saw him gave a pretty accurate picture of what she thought. Not a good omen for explanations.

Fair enough. Maybe he deserved it.

There was too much happening to do anything about it now but later he'd try to explain. It seemed his sister had come through the ordeal unscathed. He wasn't sure Sophie had—and it was his fault.

She lifted her hat off and held it in her hand as if to ward him off. The way she walked past him with her head down made him want to kick himself. He fell in behind her as she headed for the casualty room until he caught up. 'You OK?'

Sophie gritted her teeth. She was fine! Was this guy for real? 'Yes.' She didn't look at him.

'Sophie. Let me explain.'

'I'd prefer you didn't.' She stopped. 'Look. Levi. Dr Whatever-your-name-is.' That was when she realised how deep the perfidy went. 'I don't even know your last name.'

'Pearson.'

The name rang a bell. Pearson? Pearson? But she couldn't place it. She shrugged it off with a tiny shake of her head. Was it really Pearson? Who could tell with this guy?

Levi stared down at her. 'Don't you think you're being a little harsh, considering what we've been through together?'

'I really don't care if you think I'm harsh. I'm tired. I'm over this. I have to see you for the next hour but I don't have to listen. I'd appreciate it if you'd respect that.'

So they sat in the waiting room, not speaking. To start with, Sophie flicked through a magazine but every page of upmarket advertisement she turned to she imagined Levi driving that car. Eating at that restaurant. Dancing with that girl. Wearing that suit.

She threw the magazine down and leaned back in the chair and closed her eyes. She hadn't lost her heart to another city slicker. She hadn't.

Finally, after another torturous half hour, the patients were released. Odette hugged her and Smiley nodded and even put his hand on Sophie's shoulder and squeezed it.

'Thanks, Sis.'

'We were lucky,' she mumbled, and reached up and gave him a kiss. She needed to dwell on the fact that all of them were alive and that it had been pretty close. Maybe that was why she was weepy.

Sophie avoided Levi's attempt to catch her eye and she only then wondered how they were getting home. Not a helicopter, she hoped.

'I've hired a plane to get us back,' he said, as if she'd asked the question.

She risked a glance at him and he was looking at her. 'Thank you,' she mumbled but that was all.

Apparently Smiley would fly on to Xanadu to collect his vehicle and Sophie would be dropped home to sleep. First stop: Jabiru Station Township. Yes, please. Sophie couldn't wait.

The flight was short and when she finally closed her

front door behind her she leaned against it with a sigh. The wood was hard and scratchy from peeling paint and she rubbed her head against it as if to rub some sense into her brain. What had she done?

Sleep proved impossible after the events of the past two days and ridiculously the most disturbing factor was Levi's decision to keep her unaware of his profession. Maybe that was a concept which was totally ridiculous in the scheme of things but she couldn't help it.

She needed to get back to work and forget her adventures, her weakness and the high-flying people at Xanadu.

CHAPTER TEN

WHEN Sophie opened the front door the next morning she glanced across the street and Levi leant on the veranda rail of the clinic as if he owned it.

There he was. Designer jeans and Rolex flashing in the sunlight, and there she was, clutching her throat like a wimp.

She would have pulled back, hidden inside, if he hadn't straightened when he saw her, but it was too late. Too darn late.

Her hand shook as she pulled the door shut behind her and when she crossed the veranda it felt like a creek full of crocodiles were shifting underfoot. What could he possibly want? She hated that it mattered so much it made her tremble.

The dusty road, usually wide in the sunlight, seemed narrow today, and in far too little time she stood beside him. Just a drift of some expensive aftershave letting her know he was still way out of her league. 'How can I help you, Doctor?'

His eyes narrowed and when he spoke his voice was very low. 'Don't call me doctor and don't talk to me as if you don't know me.'

She blinked. Was he trying for best defence is attack? Well, she could do a little attacking of her own.

'I thought you'd be long gone.'

He sighed. 'I can see the thought of that upsets you no end.'

'Hmm.' The deserted street didn't produce any distractions so she had to look at him. 'Perhaps not.' She shrugged. Self-preservation's like that, she thought. 'Nothing personal. How can I help you?'

'I have to stay for the crash investigation team. It looks as if the chopper was definitely tampered with and there's a police investigation. I thought you should know.'

What? Ice trickled down her neck despite the heat. Deliberate sabotage? With a pregnant Odette on board? 'Tampered with? That's horrible. Who'd want to do that?' She'd no idea but it seemed the concept wasn't new to him. How surprising he hadn't shared that with her earlier.

'There's some suspicion on Steve, the resort manager. He's disappeared.'

'Steve?' She shook her head at the crazy notion. 'I don't understand.'

He ran his hand through his hair. 'It's a long story.'

Long stories take time. That meant he'd stay longer and she didn't think she could take that. 'No problem.'

She couldn't help the tiny bitterness that laced her words. She forced herself to hold out her hand and braced for that frisson she felt every time he touched her. 'All the best, then.'

He looked down at her fingers but made no move to take her hand. 'I was hoping we could part as more than friends.'

She shrugged, not without a little relief, and tucked her hand away safely by her side. She didn't want to be his special friend. They came from different worlds. Had different morals. 'I don't think so.' Blowed if she'd hold her hand out again. 'So when do you go?'

'It's taken a day to get the team in from Perth. The preliminary reports will be through late this afternoon and we leave tomorrow. I tried to send Odette back today but she refused to go without me.'

She could understand that. Especially when she'd just found out someone tried to kill her. The idea was almost too far-fetched to believe. 'She's been through a lot. I guess it would make anyone nervous to travel on their own, let alone in her circumstances.' Unconsciously she scrunched her hands inside her short pockets. Already her heart rate was palpable and she could feel the moisture on her skin—and still he hadn't come to the reason he was here.

He paused, waiting for her to ask him something, and when she didn't he went on, as if searching for a topic. So he wasn't comfortable either, she thought. Good.

'At least Odette didn't have her baby in the bush. My biggest fear. She should never have travelled so far in her pregnancy. I can't believe I didn't stop her.'

To be fair, not that she really felt like it, Sophie didn't see that. Odette was pretty much her own woman and well past the age of consent. But it was none of her business. Right?

She couldn't take much more of this. 'Why are you here?'

He stepped forward and she stepped back until her spine was against the unopened door. He cupped his fingers under her chin and gently lifted her head so that he could see straight into her face.

She wanted to shake him off but with the feel of his hand on her she lost all power. His hand was cool and firm against the heat in her skin, and his gaze captured hers as easily as when—was it only a week ago?—she'd first seen him. Despite the need to do so she couldn't look away.

Now, after the time they'd spent together, she knew his irises were rings of blue, his lashes were dark brown, not black. Memories of that time she'd felt his skin against her cheek and his mouth against hers made her shoulders droop with comfort, as if he'd done it again.

Why did he have to touch her?

Those times in Levi's arms were a whole different world—one she wasn't going to get used to—and unfortunately those few touches had been indelible. How much more proof did she need to get out? Imagine if he could read now how much she wanted to be back in his arms.

Step sideways, move away—the litany in her head drowned out his words. But her body didn't obey. Then she tried to concentrate on what he said to block out his eyes and the feel of his hand. 'I'm sorry you've been involved in this, Sophie. I'd like the chance to sit and talk before I go.'

Finally her body responded and she pulled her chin away and walked to the rail with her back to him. She couldn't sit and talk! No way. 'Was there something you wanted to ask about your sister's pregnancy?'

He came to stand beside her. 'It's nothing to do with Odette,' he said with a skyward glance of frustration. 'It's about the way we parted after extreme circumstances and I don't like that I've upset you.'

She'd have to make a good show of it. There'd be no other way to get rid of him. She held up her hands. 'Look. I don't want to talk about it. I'm over it.'

He searched her face. 'I'm not.' His scrutiny seemed almost abrasive to her skin but she blocked it out. He went on. 'What's happened to you in the past is not me. Can't you forgive me for not being more open with you?'

Nope. She was too darn scared it was the tip of the iceberg of deceit she hadn't discovered yet. Too terrified if she trusted him he would break a part of her that would never heal. She shook her head and looked back in time to a hurt that was nothing to this. 'I can't help how the past has shaped me. Men who can't tell the truth seem drawn to me. I've even a family history of being scammed by liars.'

She risked a glance at his face. 'I'm a simple girl, Levi. I say what I mean. I want you to go.'

He rubbed the back of his neck. 'What do you want me to say, Sophie? I'm sorry I misled you but there are things going on here you don't know about, and if I tell you, then you could be in danger.'

She shook her head. Not good enough. 'There's nothing more to say, then.'

He frowned at her. 'You're not giving me a chance.'

'Tough.' She shrugged her shoulders at him but they felt as heavy as if she carried a yoke with two loaded buckets. When he raised his brows at her, as though she was the one being childish, she actually felt like a child. A small one. Who'd discovered the world wasn't magical any more.

He'd tricked her just when she'd started to believe she might have found a man she could trust her heart to.

A man who warmed her when he looked at her and listened when she was off on her tangent, who stretched her mind and made her laugh and had a strong hand she could hold when she needed, and arms that comforted... All gone.

She'd thought she'd seen things in Levi that she hadn't seen in any man she'd been drawn to. But he'd dashed her fledgling hopes when he lied—the one thing she could never forgive—and she didn't have any reserves left. 'Please go.'

His face shut down until he looked like the stranger she'd seen the first day. Aloof, arrogant, then finally dismissive. 'I'm sorry you feel that way.' He turned but before he left he said, 'Where's William?'

Confusion held her answer. Smiley? 'Work. Why?' Would he never go? Her eyes stung and her throat bulged so thick with tears she could barely breathe.

'Something's come out about the family that used to own Xanadu. Do you know what their name was?'

She didn't have the energy to talk about her foolish, gullible grandfather. It was easier to say, 'No. Why?'

'Nothing important.' He took a step towards her and she panicked that she'd throw herself into his arms. She stepped back as though he'd raised his hand and her panic must have shown on her face. That stopped him.

'Goodbye, Sophie.'

He stepped off the veranda into the dust and as he walked away she realised she'd done what she'd blamed him for. She'd lied to him. And not just about her grandfather.

Levi drove back to Xanadu, too fast, which involved concentration on the road but he was grimly thankful about that. He didn't want to think. Didn't want to relive the distress he'd recognised in Sophie's eyes.

In fact, it was probably safer she wasn't seen with

him. Safer for her because he could feel the danger closing in. If the results came back as he expected it upped the ante for Steve. They were all in danger.

Two hours later Smiley burst into the clinic as Sophie sutured a nasty gash from a poorly wielded chainsaw.

The young jackaroo had been lucky he'd only touched his leg on the way through the log and had opened the skin in one thick stripe. Sophie looked up. People burst in often, but never Smiley.

She took one look at his face. 'Odette?'

'She rang me on the satellite phone. Her waters broke, and the contractions are coming every three minutes. She's refusing to move and they're at the Pentecost crossing. Then the phone died.'

That didn't make sense. 'The same spot I saw Levi the first day? Why would they go there?'

Smiley shook his head at the delay. 'It's where her father was taken.'

Her father? Taken? It all came back. Crocodiles. 'Pearson.' Levi telling her his name at Kununurra and it had rung a bell then. She couldn't believe she'd forgotten it. Such was the state Levi had her in. The name of the people her grandfather had lost the family station to. Levi hadn't been a guest; he'd been the owner. Hence, the question about her family.

Liar. No wonder they could use the choppers, drive the vehicles, do whatever they wished. Levi had lied again. She yanked the final suture through and the unfortunate young cowboy yelped in protest. Sophie bit her lip and looked at the jackaroo. 'Oops, sorry.' She tied off, snipped the ends of the suture and put a see-through dressing over the top in minimal time. 'Keep it dry. Come back in a week and I'll take the stitches out.'

The young bloke glanced at her once as if to say, *I'll take 'em out myself*, then scurried out of the room. Sophie sighed. She'd never have done that before Levi had disrupted her life.

'Xanadu.' She looked at her brother. 'They own it.' So many lies. Smiley didn't look surprised. More unpalatable truth. 'You knew?' That hurt more than anything else.

Impatiently he answered, 'Odette asked me not to say because she wasn't even supposed to tell me.'

'For goodness sake, why not?' Now these people were infecting Smiley with their subterfuge.

Smiley shook his head. 'Come on.' He gestured to the room as if to ask what do you need. 'It's not important and I really don't care. Let's go.'

Smiley drove as if driving the Dakar Rally—a man who never drove fast—and they made the crossing in an hour. A Kimberley record that Sophie never wanted to break. Her teeth rattled in her head and the dust stung her eyes but she didn't say anything. Smiley's words repeated in her head. 'It's not important and I really don't care.'

So why did she care so much when she'd been led

astray by Levi? Why did it matter in the big scheme of things? Had she overreacted? Been precious about semantics? She didn't even want to think what she could have risked if Levi really wanted to see her again.

Smiley was right. Now wasn't the time. It didn't matter. She needed to put any emotion over Levi's deceit aside and think about Odette.

She squeezed the emergency delivery pack on her lap and ran over a few scenarios. At least when she'd felt Odette's uterus the baby had palped head first and not breech, and she had medical backup in Levi, she thought bitterly.

Why wouldn't Levi just pick his sister up and move her? Surely he didn't agree with her having a baby out in the wilderness? She'd never understand these people.

When they arrived she saw why they were still there.

Levi's vehicle sat low to the ground, four flat tyres, a very reasonable excuse not to leave. The local police vehicle had pulled up next to them and the two officers were talking on the two-way.

Smiley pulled up in a shower of gravel and threw himself out of the car towards Odette, who sat with her back against a boab in her trousers and bra, and burst into tears when she saw him. Sophie blinked. That was different.

Levi sat next to her with his arm around her until Smiley took his place.

Sophie glanced back at the river, which wasn't far enough away from them, and scanned the bank. Two large saltwater crocodiles sat patiently at the edge in the shade and watched them with unblinking yellow eyes. Yikes.

Antipathy forgotten she glanced at Odette, who was lost in Smiley's arms, and turned to Levi. Her brows creased. 'You OK?'

'Will be,' he said grimly. 'Satellite phone went flat after we'd got through to the police and William.'

She frowned. He didn't look right. 'Are you hurt?'

'Stray bullet nicked me. It's nothing.' He lifted his arm from his chest and showed a wad of heavily blood-stained material tied around his left arm; she guessed it was Odette's shirt.

'Let me see.'

'Sort Odette first.' He was still giving orders. Typical.

Sophie scanned his sister quickly. She didn't sound like a woman in the final throes of labour. 'You OK, Odette?'

Odette spoke from Smiley's arms. 'I am now.'

She turned back to Levi. 'Right, now show me.'

He glared at her and held up his arm. 'We don't have time for this. He could shoot again.'

Sophie busied herself undoing the material. 'I'm assuming we're on the right side of the tree for safety.' She inclined her head towards the river. 'And that's not all who's here. The police will protect us from him but not from the couple of salties who fancy a piece of you too.'

He raised his brows at her. 'It must be your fate in life to warn me about crocodiles.'

'And yours to keep me in the dark. But we'll talk about that later.'

Gingerly he held his injured arm as she eased the wad away from the skin below his shoulder to expose a neat in hole and a less-neat out hole. The bullet had passed through in a jagged tunnel without causing major damage. Blood oozed as soon as she took the pressure away and hastily she put the wad back. He was right. It wouldn't kill him. Levi's indrawn breath made her wince. 'Sorry.'

'It's nothing. I'll heal. Get Odette away from here.'

The man was mad. 'I imagine the police will get us all away from here.'

Short sharp shake of his head and she felt her own impatience rise.

'I'm not going anywhere until I find him,' he growled.

She gestured to his shoulder. 'Not like that surely.'

'Steve, or someone, shot at us while Odette was saying goodbye. Here. Shot the tyres on the car. Tried to kill my sister. He's still out there, though the police think he's gone.' His eyes burned into hers and she shivered a little at the implacable decision to go after the shooter.

His voice lowered but was no less definite. 'I'm staying until we get him. Now, please do what I ask and take Odette. If you stay here he'll try to kill you too.'

She glanced at Smiley, who was attempting to disentangle Odette and calm her at the same time. He looked up at Sophie. 'Let's get 'em out of here.'

The bullet hit the tree beside them a millisecond before the shot rang out.

Smiley scooped Odette like she was a feather and dived around the back of the tree. Levi grabbed Sophie and pushed her behind the tree onto the ground and flattened himself on top of her. The breath whooshed from her lungs and a bunch of dead boab leaves crackled under her. The gunman had moved. She didn't want Levi to protect her with his body. Did he want to get shot again?

She sucked in another laboured breath. He was darned heavy but she doubted he'd listen to her right at this moment. Thankfully, when no further shots rang out, he eased himself off, but kept his body between her and the direction the bullet had come from.

'You all right?' he said, and she nodded. The fact that he'd cared enough to protect her made her eyes sting. Though maybe he'd have done it for any woman and she shouldn't read anything into his actions.

The hardest part was trying not to remember the feel of his strong chest against her or the male scent that reminded her of other times she'd been in his arms.

As they crouched and dusted themselves off Sophie could see a fresh splash of blood in the dirt beside her. Levi had dislodged the makeshift bandage and his wound oozed sluggishly again. 'Come here,' she said, and resettled the wadding as she frowned at him.

His eyes caught hers. 'Thank you.'

She couldn't help the heat that rode in her cheeks. 'Any time.'

He raised his brows. 'I might take you up on that.'

'This guy means business,' Smiley commented grimly when the four of them were crouched behind the thankfully wide trunk of the fat boab. The police had dived behind their own car and one of them fired back.

Levi grimaced. 'I'm so sorry you two are involved in Steve's plans.'

She looked from one man to the other. 'Involved in what plan? Now what don't I know?' Sophie demanded.

Levi sighed. 'You know the helicopter was definitely sabotaged, but I'm now convinced my father was pushed into the river here five months ago. Whoever did that is shooting at us now and I think it's my half-brother, Steve.'

She did not believe this. 'Steve's your half-brother?' This was outback Australia, not some gangland setting. Who were these people?

Levi saw her confusion. 'Because of Xanadu. It seems that my new-found half-sibling expected to inherit Xanadu, and he wants it.' He paused. 'In case we all die here…' He pulled her in close with his good arm and dropped a kiss on her lips. 'I think you are the most amazing woman I've ever met.'

He'd kissed her. In the middle of a gunfight. And by the look on his face he'd enjoyed it. Yep. He was mad. 'You must be delirious. We're being *shot at*!'

'That's why it seemed a good idea to tell you now.' He stroked her cheek. 'And I'm not lying.'

The sound of a vehicle revving and then driving

away had Smiley peer around the tree. 'Could have been someone else parked and they got scared,' Smiley said.

Levi hit the tree with the side of his fist and then winced as the vibration ran through his body to his injured arm. 'Or could be our man.'

The police car started and the officers drove off in pursuit. 'It seems the coppers agree,' Smiley said.

'Damn. Wish I'd seen the car.' Levi growled, 'Let's get the girls out of here and back to Xanadu.'

Smiley nodded, grimly, and went for the truck to reverse it back to Odette.

Sophie slid down the tree next to Odette to see how she fared. 'You OK, honey?'

The girl's head was down and she held her stomach. 'I think the baby's coming.'

She whimpered and then a tiny strangled moan had Sophie peer at her with a frown. 'We might just sit for a minute,' Sophie said to no one in particular, and rested her hand on Odette's arm. 'What's happening?'

Odette turned agonised eyes to Sophie and whispered, 'I need to go to the bathroom.'

Sophie looked at Levi. 'I think she's pushing.'

CHAPTER ELEVEN

'No. Not here.' Levi cast his eyes skywards but all he could see were the sparse leaves of the boab above him. He could handle the idea of being shot at but not the birth of Odette's baby.

He needed her safe, with doctors, and theatres, and sterile surroundings. He couldn't lose Odette like his mother. His worst nightmare. He'd failed in every aspect of keeping his sister safe. He'd involved her in a helicopter crash, a shooting and now this. He wanted her out of here and surely she could stand.

'Please stand, Odette.'

'You can't prioritise this.' Now Sophie was shaking her head at him. 'She's pushing. It's coming.'

Prioritise? He wanted his sister in a nice safe hospital. Preferably a Sydney one. How had it come to this? 'Come on, Odette. You have to get up.'

Odette looked up at him and he could see the fear behind her tremulous smile. 'Sorry. Can't do.'

He looked at Sophie and despite the sympathy he

saw in her eyes she shook her head. She was right.
Again.

The truck backed up to them and Smiley jumped out.
'Let's go.'

Levi looked helplessly down at both women, dis-
tanced from him by their silent communication.
'Sophie says Odette's having the baby.'

'She can't have it here.' Smiley cast a quick glance
to the river. 'The crocs will have the lot of us if we
don't get out.'

'Then make sure they don't,' Sophie said with a
touch of asperity. 'She'll move as soon as the baby's
born.'

'Tell the men to go away,' Odette whispered.

Sophie obliged. 'We're busy.' Smiley blinked, then
nodded and drifted away to keep watch between them
and the river. Levi looked down at this woman who'd
come into their lives and continued to cope with one
disaster after another. Thank God she was here. What
would they do without her? What would he do without
her?

When had everything changed? When had Sophie
become more important than the guilt he lived with
when he couldn't help everyone? More important than
finding his father's killer. More important to protect
than himself. Was she his unforeseen destiny?

Sophie and Odette leaned with their backs against
the tree. 'You concentrate on listening to your body and
I'll worry about everything else. Just breathe it out,' she

said quietly and looked up at him. 'I need the kit out of the truck and the rugs I brought, please.' At least it seemed he could be of use.

He did as requested and then returned with what she'd asked. 'Where do you want it?'

'Spread around us and the thin rug over Odette. And pass me the pack and the towel. Thanks.' She helped Odette adjust her clothing under the rug, then undid the delivery pack and laid the cord clamps aside. She drew up the Syntocinon for after the birth, washed her hands with antiseptic, then pulled on the gloves. 'A little primitive but this tree has great facilities compared to the camp the other day.'

Levi strangled back an inappropriate laugh. He supposed it did and he watched her lean back against the tree next to his sister and wait. Her capable hands were clasped loosely on her lap. As if just another April day in the Kimberleys. How was he ever going to go back to Sydney and leave her? Except for the minor fact she wouldn't have him.

Odette looked up once, an arrested expression on her face as she stared at Sophie. 'William said you told him birthing a baby was like having a foal or a calf.'

Sophie brushed the hair off Odette's forehead with her finger and smiled. She had a great smile, Levi thought as he pretended not to listen.

'He's a bad boy for repeating that. I said that because he was scared for you. But you're doing so well it might be true.'

Levi saw the tears well as Odette sniffed. 'I want to go home. I can't believe it's happening here.' His fault.

'After meeting you two?' Sophie rolled her eyes and she glanced at him quickly before looking back at Odette. 'I can.'

Odette's laugh was cut short by the next pain and Levi winced as it dragged a low groan from her as the baby moved down.

Levi twisted his hands; he felt so damn powerless to do anything for either of them.

'Beautiful,' said Sophie in that quiet, almost hypnotic voice he'd never be able to match in the circumstances. 'Slow breaths. Not long now.'

She looked up and frowned when she saw him watching her. He stretched his lips into a strained smile but she must have seen his tension. 'Take a few breaths too, Levi. It's OK.'

He was always in trouble with this woman. 'Can I get you anything, Sophie?'

'Sip of water, for Odette, thanks. There's a bottle in the truck. And maybe check on Smiley.' In other words, his marching orders. OK. Maybe he would be better out of the way until it was all over.

'Call him William!' Odette mumbled through gritted teeth, as she finished the pain and breathed out.

Levi handed her the water and drifted away and Sophie watched him go. He appeared unflappable considering the day he'd had and that his sister was doing what he'd dreaded all along. Sophie couldn't guarantee everything would be fine; she could just assume it would, and deal with the variations as they came.

And Levi would be there for support if she needed him. She had enormous faith in him and she didn't quite know where it had grown from. He'd become a good person to have around. She could've become used to that.

Odette gripped her hand and Sophie refocused where she should have been all along.

Odette panted and bit her lip. 'I don't think I want to do this.'

Sophie closed her fingers around Odette's shoulder in support. 'I know. Let it happen. Just push your tummy out as you breathe in, and let it fall as you breathe out, and the baby will move down.'

Odette breathed and finally Sophie could see the first signs of descent. 'I can see some dark hair now, Odette, so he's not bald.'

Odette's eyes stared into hers as she searched Sophie's face. 'The contraction's gone and it's burning.'

'As it should,' Sophie said quietly. 'Everything needs to stretch and the head sitting there is the best way to do that.'

'I am so not doing this again,' Odette ground out as she panted the pain away. Then her voice changed. 'Can I touch him?'

Sophie smiled—she loved this bit—and took her hand to guide it down to the baby's head. 'Of course.'

Odette stretched tentatively until she realised there

was a hard little scalp right under her fingers and her hand jumped away. 'Oh, my Lord. This is so not right.'

'Afraid it is.' Sophie smiled. 'The next pain will move baby out more, just remember to push slowly with your breath. You don't want your baby to come out too fast.'

'I don't?' She whistled her breath in between her teeth. 'You've got to be kidding.' Odette closed her eyes and breathed, and by fractions the baby descended.

Sophie stroked Odette's hair out of her eyes. 'You are amazing, you know that?'

The next contraction built and the amount of the baby's head grew slowly as Odette breathed him out. Wrinkled forehead, eyes and nose, and finally mouth and chin, until the whole head rotated to face his mother's leg. Sophie dried the little face and hair gently as they waited for the next contraction.

'He's blinking,' she told Odette.

Odette panted. 'But his body's not out.'

'He's awake, that's for sure.' And as Odette pushed for the last time, the baby eased into Sophie's hands. She ran the towel over him as he opened his eyes wider—a dark, dark blue—and he blinked as he looked around.

'It really is a boy? I have my son?' Then, 'He's not crying,' Odette said as Sophie slid him up his mother's body skin to skin until he lay across Odette's breasts. She covered them both with the rug and tucked the edges in.

'He doesn't have to, he's breathing. He's pink and happy to be on you. And yes, he's definitely a boy.'

Sophie gave the injection, clamped and cut the cord and waited for the third stage to complete. When it was over she checked Odette's uterus through her soft belly skin, and found it rocklike beneath her fingers. Everything had done as it should. She pulled the rug back again and checked Odette's pulse.

'It's over.' Odette smiled up at her. 'I've done it.' Her smile seemed to light up ten feet around them. She glanced down at her son. 'I can't tell you how having you here helped me do that.'

'My privilege.' They sat there quietly for a minute or two. Just breathing and allowing the peace of the bush to steal over them. To appreciate the wonder of childbirth in such a primitive setting. The baby squirmed and Odette laughed and stroked his head and she glanced at Sophie. Their eyes met and they both smiled.

'Can you ask Levi and William to come see him now, please?' The softness in those powerful new mother's eyes made it hard for Sophie to swallow and her eyes stung. This was why she loved this job.

'Sure.' Sophie tucked a little escaping hand back under the blankets around Odette's new son and stripped off her gloves. 'Congratulations. You were amazing.'

'Thank you, Sophie. I just let you worry about everything else.' She stroked the downy head as her son wrinkled his forehead and blinked up at her. 'He's so gorgeous.'

Sophie stroked his tiny hand that escaped again and nodded. She signalled Levi over and watched the men fuss over mother and baby. Her face ached with a broad goofy smile that faded with just a tinge of melancholy for what might have been. She walked towards the river to keep watch.

A few minutes later Levi stood and crossed the grass to her side and she moved back to a safer distance. He smiled ruefully, and then stepped forward and deliberately eased in closer to invade her space. 'You are getting a hug whether you like it or not.'

'Oh.' She didn't know what to say to that, and in the end she didn't have to say anything as Levi lifted his good arm and drew her against his chest. She sighed against him. She was glad he insisted, she thought as she sighed again.

'Thank you, Sophie,' he said quietly, and they stood there, with the sound of the river gurgling behind them and the raucous laugh of a kookaburra punctuating their isolation.

His arm was warm and heavy around her shoulders and the amount of comfort she gained was disproportionate to the gesture. She leant her head more heavily against the good side of his body for a few precious seconds and allowed her facial bones to savour the hardness of his chest against her cheek, the feel of his shirt against her skin and to hear his heart beat, like a rhythmic drum that beat out a cadence of support.

She'd never really been a girl to lean on people. Hadn't really learnt how until now. There was something magic about the way Levi could remove weariness from her like a blanket lifting from her shoulders. He could energise her with a look, let alone the circle of his arms. Shame she'd refused to listen to him when she'd had the chance.

Her nose wrinkled. She could smell his blood. She focused on the damp patch a few inches from her nose and it was as if a beam of stark white light had been switched on in her brain. Her stupid brain that hadn't seen it all before while she'd been distracted by Odette's need. How could she have missed it? Like a splash of cold water from the river, the concept of Levi's death stared at her, shocking and far too real. It had been that close.

He could have died. Been dead right now. The reality squeezed her chest and her throat closed over. She'd been the greatest fool. Imagine if the bullet had been a few inches closer to his heart. For the first time she realised how narrow her escape...to losing the man she suddenly couldn't doubt she loved. Why had it taken her so long to realise?

She loved him. The tears prickled then, and stung, and burned at the thought of Levi in mortal danger. She'd been obsessing about his perceived faults to protect her own realisation. Of course she loved him. What had she been thinking?

'So here we are again,' he said into her hair, and the vibration, more poignant for his mortality, felt so much more precious than her own pride. If he'd been dead she'd have missed this. Any of this. All of this. Oblivious to her epiphany he went on musingly. 'I thought I'd seen the last of you.'

Thank God he hadn't. She closed her eyes and two fat tears ran down her cheeks. She swallowed and tried to level her voice. 'Fate conspires apparently.'

'Hmm,' he rumbled beneath her. 'Unfortunately, fate wasn't the only one conspiring. I'm sorry you and William were involved in this mess.'

Then she remembered she'd lied to him too and she hadn't told him. Suddenly it was so hard to start. Funny that. After all her bluster about being kept in the dark and offence at the misconceptions he'd practised, she'd done the same.

'Congratulations on your nephew,' she said weakly as she pulled away. She turned to surreptitiously wipe her cheeks.

'Lucky baby to have a new beginning,' he went on drily, and she could feel his eyes follow her as she widened the distance.

New beginnings. Could she do that? 'What would you do with a new beginning if you had one?' She took her eyes off the bank in front of them to look back at his face. Maybe they could laugh about the irony.

She didn't see the grey crocodile move a foot closer to where they stood on the gravel. The whole world had condensed down to Levi—the fact that she wanted to run back to his arms and didn't know if she could go through life denying that she'd had the chance and blew it. Now she'd stopped lying to herself.

Motionless, the huge crocodile watched her with unblinking yellow eyes and even Levi didn't see the danger until the reptile moved again.

Levi must have sensed or seen the sweep of the jagged tail out of the corner of his eye as the crocodile moved because he caught Sophie's hand and pulled her back into his arms and back towards the truck. 'Let's go. The crocs are getting hungry.' She'd forgotten the danger again. When she'd promised herself she never would. Far too close for comfort.

Levi pulled her to him. 'My turn to warn you.'

His hand was tight around her wrist, painfully so, as he shuffled them both backed towards the tree and Sophie glanced back. 'Too close,' she said as she shuddered.

'Time to go, William,' he called over his shoulder, and all Sophie could think about was the way her dog had died and the fact that she'd forgotten her own rules. She was the one who was supposed to know the dangers. When she leant up against the truck her legs trembled and threatened to collapse. They both could have been killed. She shuddered again and he gathered her up and put her on the seat.

They both looked back and the crocodile had stopped in the spot they'd been standing. His thick reptilian tail swayed back and forth in frustration. His mate left the water and came to stand beside him.

Smiley whistled as he gathered the belongings and helped Odette move with her baby to the truck. 'We need to relocate those fellows,' Smiley said. 'Before they wipe your whole family out.'

'And yours,' said Levi grimly.

Smiley shook his head. 'Never seen 'em so nasty. It's not normal.'

'Spare me from feeling sorry for the crocodile.' Levi stared at the water. 'Though I wonder if that was planned too? Steve could have been feeding them. Knowing Odette wanted to put a plaque up here.'

'If they don't catch him we'll never know.'

It was a subdued party that returned to Xanadu. Smiley drove, and the others crammed like sardines, with Odette's baby, into the front. Sophie sat on Levi and his arms held her as if he'd never let her go. Considering the day, Sophie was more than happy with that.

Levi drew her into the resort building with his arm still protectively pulling her against him. Every now and then her mind recapped the morning, dwelling on Levi's close escape. 'I need to see to your wound before we go.'

He frowned. 'It's nothing. We'll get Odette settled first and get you a stiff drink.' He signalled to one of the indoor staff.

She was over the crocodile. It was the shooting that knocked her. Levi could have died. 'Fine. But I'm not leaving until I've had a good look.'

He glanced at her as he waited to be put through to the police. 'Think about yourself for a change.' She watched him organise Odette, call the police—where he learned Steve had been placed in custody—then break the news to the staff of Steve's involvement.

She should be dressing his wound, not watching him direct the world. 'Can't you do this later?'

He smiled down at her, and the way even that brief lift of his lips affected her heart was enough to warn her how bad it would be when he'd gone. 'What will you do when you don't have me to boss around?' he said.

Not what she wanted to dwell on. 'Be lonely, I guess.' She said it more to herself than to him and she didn't see his arrested expression. 'I'll find some first-aid gear.' She began to move off and he caught her hand. Like he had that night they first came here, only this time her hand seemed to tangle in his as her fingers clasped his back.

'Wait. Sophie.' He looked around and ushered her, not resisting for once, through the door and out onto the veranda and down the steps to the rustic bench under the massive boab.

He stared into her face and this time there was nowhere to hide. 'What did you mean? "Be lonely"?'

Could she do it? Throw it all away or be brave? The fear was there. The risk of pain greater than anything she'd experienced, but today's close shaves had taught her a valuable lesson. She had to take that risk. 'I'll be lonely without you.' She looked back at him. That strong jaw, that mouth—the man who'd stormed into her heart when she'd been kicking and screaming the whole way, and he'd achieved it so easily in such a short time. 'I must have become used to having you around. In a week.' She laughed mirthlessly at her foolishness.

It was too late to deny a recognition on a different level and that something in him called to her the way no other person did. She saw the trappings of wealth she'd said she despised and the bender of truth when she'd promised she'd never listen to another lie. But she'd also seen the man who completed her. Who instinctively knew when she needed support and gave unstintingly.

No one had ever understood her before. That was the crux. Levi got her. Knew where she was coming from almost before she did. 'Why is that?'

'Why is what?' he said, and she realised she must have asked out loud.

'Why do you seem to understand me when others don't?'

His voice softened. 'If you tried, you could understand me too.' When she looked into his eyes she saw him clearly, as if through a fresh pane of glass, unmarked by what had come in the past.

His caring, readiness to learn new things, listen to her point of view. His willingness to be there when the burden became too much, his hand there to pull her up and his arms to comfort. Maybe she did understand him in ways she'd never wanted to understand others. And finally, with tiny tentative steps, she allowed herself to glimpse what life with Levi could be like. If she allowed herself to trust him.

Was it that easy? 'Maybe I understand you a little.'

He slipped his good arm around her. 'Two people, from opposite ends of a huge country, meet and share extraordinary events. We've both changed, shared things—perhaps it's meant to be.'

She shook her head. It was all so confusing. 'How can it be meant when you live somewhere I could never live?'

He smiled. 'And vice versa.'

Hopeless case. She'd known it. 'See.'

'We will. In time.' He hugged her and stood to help her up. 'Come on. You need to rest after all this excitement. It's been a big day.' He touched her cheek. 'But we're not finished with this subject.'

Then she remembered. If she was going to be brave she may as well finish it. 'And there's something I have to tell you.'

He stopped. 'Really?' He searched her face, frowned and then slowly he smiled. 'Do I detect a hint of guilt?'

She blushed and he laughed. His eyes opened wide with amusement. 'Oh. I hope so. From Miss Trustworthy herself?' She didn't say anything and he pulled her back down on the seat.

She tried to stand again but he kept hold of her hand and she subsided. 'I'm not rushing this,' he said. 'This is priceless. Do go on.'

She ducked her chin, suddenly shy, then resolutely raised it. 'You know when you asked if I knew the original family from Xanadu?'

'Hmm.'

Why did it feel as if he were watching her face more than listening to her words. 'Pay attention. I'm feeling bad here.'

He squeezed her shoulders. 'Good. You look very cute when you're guilty.'

'I told you I didn't know—' she drew a deep breath '—but I do. I lied. It was my grandfather. Oh, and Smiley's grandfather. Our father's father.'

He laughed. 'You lied to me?'

She looked away. 'It was such a long story—I didn't want to talk about it then.' How dare he laugh at her.

'You lied.'

She glared. 'Not as many times as you did but there is a certain irony.'

'Brilliantly so.' He tilted his head and he wasn't smiling. 'But I don't think I can talk to you any more. I'm too hurt that you deceived me.'

She frowned, frozen for a moment in time that she'd offended him deeply, then realised he'd teased her. She glared at him. 'So under all that moody exterior you're a comedian?'

'Moody? Never. Work worn.' He kissed her. 'And you have to admit, you not telling the truth is hilariously funny.'

She glared at him again but he'd moved on musingly. 'So Sullivan was his name. Your grandfather? You and Smiley are the true owners of Xanadu?'

In another life. 'No.'

He tilted his head as he worked it out. 'But my grandfather cheated at cards and documented it. Was, in fact, very proud of scamming your grandfather out of his birthright.'

Her foolish grandfather had lost it though. 'Nice genes you have, Dr Pearson.'

He winked at her. 'I'm working on that.'

What was that supposed to mean? 'Anyway, whatever he wrote, it's not legal.'

'Another thing we'll discuss later.'

There was that money issue. She wished she could get over it. 'Are you very well off?'

He didn't smile but she could see the flicker of amusement at her prejudice. 'Afraid so. Stinking rich. Grandfather tripled the family coffers in his day and I've made some pretty useful investments too.'

'Oh.' He seemed so different to Brad. 'You still work hard to help others though. When financially you don't need to do anything?'

'I need to for me. I'm not proud of my father or grandfather. Never a thought to benefit their fellow man. When my brother died I vowed I'd make him proud of me. Do some good.'

She savoured the way he looked down at her. As if she'd lightened his day just by being there. No one had looked at her like that since her parents had died. 'You seem so different from when you came.'

'Am I? Then you've made me so. I've been beating myself up for the past two years and had forgotten how to smile. A certain determined young midwife has made me realise there is more to life than regretting what can't be changed.'

'What couldn't be changed?' She needed to know. Needed to see what had formed this man she'd grown to love. To try, if she could, to help him. 'What hurt you? Tell me.'

'The loss of one of my patients. I blamed myself.'

'She died in an operation?'

'No, Miss Impatient. She didn't die in an operation. None of my patients have died in their operations.'

'Sorr-ry.' He wrinkled his brow at her and she realised she'd been distracted by his rebuke. But he was still smiling at her. Then his smile departed and she could see the sadness.

'The day we confirmed there was nothing I could do to restore her sight she stepped in front of a truck.'

Sophie drew a sharp breath. Of course that would affect him. 'Like your brother. That was probably an accident too, you know,' she said earnestly. She saw the pain he still held and she squeezed his hand and her heart lifted when he squeezed back. She was glad to offer even that tiny comfort.

'It was no accident.' He went on. 'It hit home and I blamed myself.' He shrugged. 'Maybe there'd been something I could have tried. Should I have encour-aged more strongly her hope for the future of technology?' He shook his head over a tragedy that could never be rectified. 'It's too late for her but I've doubled my workload. Tried to help more people until even my colleagues were telling me to take a break.'

She understood the concept of never doing enough. Had run herself ragged since returning to the Kimberleys but for a different reason. 'You can't help the whole world.'

'When my father died suddenly, things in his will puzzled me. I'd thought he hated me, but I regretted I'd never tried to sway him towards a more fulfilling life. Grown up enough to talk to him, perhaps?'

Sophie squeezed the hand holding hers. 'People die unexpectedly and we regret what we didn't say. We all do.'

'I know I do,' he said, and gave her a thank-you-for-understanding smile, and she felt her heart expand with his pain.

One thing she didn't understand. 'But your father died five months ago. Why so long before you came here?'

He shrugged. 'I had to clear the backlog of cases I'd promised. And wait for the wet season to finish.' His gaze brushed over her and the glow in his eyes when he did so made her blush. 'I wish I'd come earlier.'

Imagine that. She'd have been in Perth and missed knowing him. Even if he broke her heart now she could never regret that she met him. Had grown from knowing him in ways she'd never believe. 'Then lucky you didn't because I wouldn't have been here.'

He smiled down at her. 'Fate.'

'Serendipitous.' She snuggled under his arm, reluctant for this camaraderie to end. She'd learnt so much that helped her understand.

'Sophie.' He spoke into her hair.

She sighed. Soaking the moment in, in case it was the last time. 'What?'

'Look at me.'

He lifted his arm and she sat back and turned to face him. Her eyes met his and what she saw in them made the breath jam in her throat.

He lifted her hand and kissed her wrist. 'I see in you all the good things I wanted to find in myself. Things I find precious and uplifting and make me want to be a better man.'

She shook her head. She hadn't done anything.

Then he took both her hands in his and squeezed her fingers. 'I've come to know you—and love you.' Her breath caught in her throat but he went on. 'I can't imagine going home without you. I can't imagine anywhere without you.'

She searched his face, not believing his words, but unable to stop the sudden gallop in her chest. He couldn't love her.

She looked again and this time became a little less unconvinced as she saw the confirmation in his eyes. 'What are you saying?'

He smiled down at her. Like he really did love her? She hugged that impossible thought tightly as hope began to build. 'Will you marry me? Be my partner for life?' He lifted her hand to his mouth and kissed her palm, then folded her fingers over his salute. 'Can you love me back?'

She reached up and stroked his face. Those strong lines of cheek and jaw with the first regrowth of dark whiskers bristly beneath her fingers. How had she found him? Been so fortunate? Her eyes stung and she chewed her lip, suddenly too frightened to say the words out loud. She took a deep breath and then she did.

'I already love you. Too much. Apparently since the waterhole on our trek. The moment you reached down to lift me. And then you kissed me and nothing was the same again.' She remembered the instant. 'I was so frightened you'd hurt me again I wasn't game to let the feeling out. And now you've exposed me.' Her eyes filled with happy tears. 'So, yes, please. I'll be your wife.'

Levi looked down at her. 'So you'll keep me on the straight and narrow?' He gestured to the gorge below them. 'Even away from your beloved Kimberleys?'

She shrugged. Suddenly home wasn't home if Levi wasn't there. 'We can visit.'

Levi barely dared to believe he wasn't going to lose her. Sophie's beautiful face turned up at him, so sincere and open and honest and shining with love. How had he been this blessed? His throat tightened and he pulled her close and held her against his heart as the world receded. His Sophie. His heart. His love. The other stuff they'd work out.

CHAPTER TWELVE

SOPHIE gazed around at the guests at their wedding, an unlikely mix of smiling faces, as the setting sun dusted the rugged ranges in the distance a glowing and loving lilac. Loving like the vows she and Levi had exchanged above the stunning gorge at Xanadu and glowing like the look in her new husband's eyes.

She smiled at her friends—the sun-frocked women, and their sun-browned men in best Akubras and polished boots—and Levi's friends in the sprinkling of suits and designer dresses, and the way the two groups melded with much gaiety under the leafless branches of the giant boab.

A tree that had grown more bulbous over the thousand years it had stood under a blue Kimberley sky and watched each turn of fortune this grand old homestead had seen since it had been built by her great-grandfather and lost for two generations. Now her and Levi's children, and maybe Smiley and Odette's children,

FIONA MCARTHUR 179

would visit, and one day those growing children would learn to love their heritage.

The cries of sulphur-crested cockatoos filled the late-afternoon air and she lifted her head to allow the noise to soak into her memory as she inhaled the delicate aroma of the frangipani called Kimberley Gold in her bouquet. The heady scent enveloped the wedding party better than any designer fragrance yet to be fashioned by man.

She'd be fine in the city. Beside her stood Levi, her husband, so tall and straight and gazing down at her with such a look of pride and love in his dark blue eyes the tears pricked behind the mascara that Odette had insisted she wear, and she had to force her fingers not to rub her eyes.

He must have seen the glitter she tried to hide because his thumb gently rubbed her palm in comfort. Already he knew what she was thinking, and magically the tears receded as his fingers entwined through hers. He looked down at the impressive pink Kimberley diamond ring they'd chosen from the mine and she tutted as she followed his gaze. 'You have too much money.'

He smiled. 'Would you like me to give it all away?' The words were spoken lightly but the look in his eyes assured her he was deadly serious, and her heart thumped at the lengths this man would go to make her happy.

She blinked back more tears, refusing to weep even tears of joy on her wedding day. 'I could help you.' She smiled up at him. 'There's lots of things I'd like to improve around here.' *Even if I'm not here to see them*, she thought, with barely any regret.

He hugged her to him. 'I can see I've taken on an expensive wife.' She felt his arm around her, so strong and sure of their love, and the truth was there to see. This was home. In Levi's arms. Not Xanadu, not busy Sydney, or wherever his work took him—anywhere was home as long as she had Levi by her side.

The small plane—Levi had declined the helicopter with a smiling glance at his new wife—flew out the next morning, and with his hand in hers Sophie watched the brown earth pass beneath her with no regrets. The timeless mountains and steep-sided gorges would be there for ever. Xanadu would stand watch over the land until she returned.

Now she could look to the future and new adventures with the man she trusted with all her heart.

That night in Sydney they dined at an exclusive restaurant overlooking Sydney Harbour and Sophie could see why Levi loved it.

'This used to be my favourite place to eat,' Levi said as he gazed around at the panoramic harbour views and then back at his wife. Then he looked down at his plate and somehow she knew he was thinking of their bush-tucker walk through the hot bush. 'You've broadened my palate.'

'Do they serve grubs here?' she teased, and stretched her hand out across the fine white tablecloth to his. A frisson of magic passed between them and curved her lips in that persistent secret smile she'd had since last night. How could she not have known what had awaited her in Levi's arms? Yet what could have prepared her for the experience Levi had created as he'd shown her the meaning of giving and taking in all that love had to offer. Still her skin tingled and quivered as even a fleeting touch like this brought back memories and sensations she'd never imagined, and their rings glinted as their fingers entwined.

His eyes smouldered and she felt her belly kick. 'You're blushing, my wife,' he teased.

Sophie fanned herself. 'Must be the food.'

'Strange, how the food is the last thing I'm thinking of. For you I would even eat a witchetty grub.'

Thank goodness this restaurant was discreet but she needed to change the subject before her wicked husband said something even more outrageous. Sophie poked at the delicacies he'd ordered for her. 'I won't ask you if you don't make me eat that oyster.'

He laughed and took the morsel from her plate. 'I've something better for you.' She frowned as he reached into the pocket of his suit and withdrew a long white envelope.

Thick and embossed, he placed it in her hand with such an air of expectation she frowned.

'To my darling wife with love.' For a fleeting moment the weight of the paper sent an echo of mistrust and dread left from her dealings with Brad, but she banished it easily with her unswerving knowledge of Levi's love. Now what had he thought up?

She frowned down at the envelope and then back at him. 'What's this?' She weighed it in her hand and the thickness of paper folded had her intrigued.

'Open it.'

She tried, but it was sealed and stubborn, and Levi smiled as he handed her a knife to slit the edge. She glanced across at him. Whatever it was, he was enjoying this. Finally the envelope opened and she eased the thick wad of paper out and unfolded it.

It couldn't be! Her eyes widened as she moistened suddenly dry lips.

'A million acres?' She looked at him again and his blue eyes danced with amusement and love. 'You can't give me a million acres for a wedding present.'

He sat back to enjoy the view more. 'Why not?'

'It's too much.' She looked up at him. Not sure how he'd take the next thought. 'I'd want to give Smiley half.'

He grinned. Well pleased with himself. 'I thought you'd say that, but he's agreed to be bought out.'

She frowned. 'Xanadu needs managing. We're living in Sydney.'

He raised his brows. 'Perhaps we should only live in Sydney six months of the year.'

He was enjoying this. Stringing her along. But she couldn't help the excitement that grew with each tumbled thought. 'And where will we be the rest of the time?'

'Guess.' He lifted her hand and ran his fingers along

the soft skin before he gently, and so reverently that her face flamed, kissed her wrist. 'Let's spend that money you said I should give away.'

'By buying out Smiley?'

He shook his head and kissed her again and she watched the gooseflesh rise on her arms. She wished he wouldn't do that now because concentration was hard and she wanted to understand.

'By buying an outback eye clinic. The Sophie Pearson Mobile Eye Clinic, in fact.' He smiled. 'You'll be pleased to know it's made quite a dent in our wealth.'

She shook her head, overwhelmed by his vision, but he hadn't finished. 'I thought, if you agree, we'd travel north and visit out-flung camps and missions during the dry, from May till October, and work together.'

She saw the passion in his eyes. The chance to do good work. She felt the tears well at her own fortune in finding a man she could be so proud of.

She tilted her head and she'd bet there was the same excitement shining from her own eyes that she could see in his. 'Of course, we'll need a base to work from and Xanadu fits the bill perfectly.'

She struggled to hold back her tears as she tried to take in the vision he'd created. 'Funny that.'

'And should you become otherwise engaged—' he glanced wickedly down at her narrow waist '—I can hire an assistant while you wait at home with our family, at Xanadu.'

He'd done this for her. 'You've thought of everything.'

His eyes darkened and she blushed right down to her toes and in all the places he'd discovered last night. 'And if we have children they will grow to love both homes.'

The warmth he created just by looking at her expanded until she could feel herself glow. 'You really have thought of everything.'

'I just follow the rule.' He leaned across and kissed her lips. 'Always tell the truth. And the truth is, I will love my darling wife for ever and ever.'

MILLS & BOON®

JUNE 2010 HARDBACK TITLES

ROMANCE

Marriage: To Claim His Twins	Penny Jordan
The Royal Baby Revelation	Sharon Kendrick
Under the Spaniard's Lock and Key	Kim Lawrence
Sweet Surrender with the Millionaire	Helen Brooks
The Virgin's Proposition	Anne McAllister
Scandal: His Majesty's Love-Child	Annie West
Bride in a Gilded Cage	Abby Green
Innocent in the Italian's Possession	Janette Kenny
The Master of Highbridge Manor	Susanne James
The Power of the Legendary Greek	Catherine George
Miracle for the Girl Next Door	Rebecca Winters
Mother of the Bride	Caroline Anderson
What's A Housekeeper To Do?	Jennie Adams
Tipping the Waitress with Diamonds	Nina Harrington
Saving Cinderella!	Myrna Mackenzie
Their Newborn Gift	Nikki Logan
The Midwife and the Millionaire	Fiona McArthur
Knight on the Children's Ward	Carol Marinelli

HISTORICAL

Rake Beyond Redemption	Anne O'Brien
A Thoroughly Compromised Lady	Bronwyn Scott
In the Master's Bed	Blythe Gifford

MEDICAL™

From Single Mum to Lady	Judy Campbell
Children's Doctor, Shy Nurse	Molly Evans
Hawaiian Sunset, Dream Proposal	Joanna Neil
Rescued: Mother and Baby	Anne Fraser

MILLS & BOON

JUNE 2010 LARGE PRINT TITLES

ROMANCE

The Wealthy Greek's Contract Wife — Penny Jordan
The Innocent's Surrender — Sara Craven
Castellano's Mistress of Revenge — Melanie Milburne
The Italian's One-Night Love-Child — Cathy Williams
Cinderella on His Doorstep — Rebecca Winters
Accidentally Expecting! — Lucy Gordon
Lights, Camera…Kiss the Boss — Nikki Logan
Australian Boss: Diamond Ring — Jennie Adams

HISTORICAL

The Rogue's Disgraced Lady — Carole Mortimer
A Marriageable Miss — Dorothy Elbury
Wicked Rake, Defiant Mistress — Ann Lethbridge

MEDICAL™

Snowbound: Miracle Marriage — Sarah Morgan
Christmas Eve: Doorstep Delivery — Sarah Morgan
Hot-Shot Doc, Christmas Bride — Joanna Neil
Christmas at Rivercut Manor — Gill Sanderson
Falling for the Playboy Millionaire — Kate Hardy
The Surgeon's New-Year Wedding Wish — Laura Iding

0 Gen Std HB

JULY 2010 HARDBACK TITLES

ROMANCE

A Night, A Secret...A Child	Miranda Lee
His Untamed Innocent	Sara Craven
The Greek's Pregnant Lover	Lucy Monroe
The Mélendez Forgotten Marriage	Melanie Milburne
Sensible Housekeeper, Scandalously Pregnant	Jennie Lucas
The Bride's Awakening	Kate Hewitt
The Devil's Heart	Lynn Raye Harris
The Good Greek Wife?	Kate Walker
Propositioned by the Billionaire	Lucy King
Unbuttoned by Her Maverick Boss	Natalie Anderson
Australia's Most Eligible Bachelor	Margaret Way
The Bridesmaid's Secret	Fiona Harper
Cinderella: Hired by the Prince	Marion Lennox
The Sheikh's Destiny	Melissa James
Vegas Pregnancy Surprise	Shirley Jump
The Lionhearted Cowboy Returns	Patricia Thayer
Dare She Date the Dreamy Doc?	Sarah Morgan
Neurosurgeon . . . and Mum!	Kate Hardy

HISTORICAL

Vicar's Daughter to Viscount's Lady	Louise Allen
Chivalrous Rake, Scandalous Lady	Mary Brendan
The Lord's Forced Bride	Anne Herries

MEDICAL™

Dr Drop-Dead Gorgeous	Emily Forbes
Her Brooding Italian Surgeon	Fiona Lowe
A Father for Baby Rose	Margaret Barker
Wedding in Darling Downs	Leah Martyn

MILLS & BOON

JULY 2010 LARGE PRINT TITLES

ROMANCE

Greek Tycoon, Inexperienced Mistress — Lynne Graham
The Master's Mistress — Carole Mortimer
The Andreou Marriage Arrangement — Helen Bianchin
Untamed Italian, Blackmailed Innocent — Jacqueline Baird
Outback Bachelor — Margaret Way
The Cattleman's Adopted Family — Barbara Hanna
Oh-So-Sensible Secretary — Jessica Hart
Housekeeper's Happy-Ever-After — Fiona Harper

HISTORICAL

One Unashamed Night — Sophia James
The Captain's Mysterious Lady — Mary Nichol
The Major and the Pickpocket — Lucy Ashford

MEDICAL™

Posh Doc, Society Wedding — Joanna Nei
The Doctor's Rebel Knight — Melanie Milburne
A Mother for the Italian's Twins — Margaret McDonagh
Their Baby Surprise — Jennifer Taylor
New Boss, New-Year Bride — Lucy Clark
Greek Doctor Claims His Bride — Margaret Barker